CURSED
GIFT

LEONARD F.
MORRISSEY

TABLE OF CONTENTS

CHAPTER 1

Leah Jessica held her melting sprinkled vanilla ice cream tightly in both hands. She was fixated on her father arguing with a man who was shining like a bright bulb.

Just two hours before, Leah, as she liked to be called, arrived at the largest event of the year in Louisville, KY. It was July 4th and the premier annual town event was pure family fun and a kid's dreamland consisting of games, pony rides, a farmers' market and wonderful fried food. Leah's most cherished day of the year had finally arrived, and despite her tender age of ten, she had diligently circled the date on the calendar for a full year. It was *her* day.

When her parents, Betty and Travis, stopped the car on the grass before the walk-in entrance, Leah boiling in excitement asked, "Mom, can we go now?".

"Yes dear. Let us grab our things, but don't get out of the car just yet."

Though still young, she had understood her mother to be deeply caring yet very careful. Mom was always telling her to be look both ways and do not talk to strangers. She loved her mom.

"Hey sweety, are you looking forward to an awesome day?"

Leah looked at her dad and smiled widely. She was her dad's biggest fan. He was kind, smiled a lot, and never seemed to get upset or mad. He was her hero.

"Daddy, can we get ice cream?"

"Absolutely. But let's wait just a little bit and look around. That way we'll be good and thirsty and we'll be even more excited when we get it!"

Her dad had a way of making her ok with waiting for the good stuff.

"Ok!" she beamed.

They had made their way around the mostly grassy complex, looking at chickens and lambs, taking a small pony ride around a circle and marveling at magicians doing simple magical tricks. It was everything and more than Leah had expected and remembered.

"Ready for the ice cream yet?"

Leah did not have to be told. She grabbed her dad's hand first and then her mom's and pulled them both quickly towards the large ice cream stand. It was fronted by a towering plastic cone and surprisingly had few people yet in the lineup. She was thrilled.

"Can I have vanilla please?"

"With lots of sprinkles too!" Her dad beat her to the punch. She playfully punched him in the arm.

The server handed Leah hers first and she walked to a bench near the stand. She could sense her mom eying her, and that made her fer safe. She was mesmerized by the size of the cone. Her world shrunk to a bubble that consisted of her sprinkled cone and taste buds. She was careful not to spill any on herself but reveled in the moment.

"Get the hell out of the way!"

Leah heard a man scream. She looked up slightly confused and wondered who could be yelling in a paradise like this. After a quick scan, she noticed her mom frozen stiff and her dad talking to a man that was shining bright; though she did not really understand how or why. It resembled the light that shined on the lead actor in one of her school plays. Her mom and dad seemed to be in a shadow. Leah was confused.

"Please sir, just calm down." She could see her father was agitated but in a manner that was warm and not angry. He had both hands up in the air as if to say everything's fine. Leah understood this. Many times played cops and robbers and her dad would always surrender this way when she caught him.

"Get your goddamn hands out of my face?" The man grew brighter.

Shaken, Leah looked at her mom who had still not moved - she looked terrified. She noticed her mom's hand was on her dad's waist as if to stop him from moving forward. Leah had not noticed the vanilla was beginning to drip on her yellow sun dress.

"Sir, we're just paying for our ice cream and we'll be leaving. We'll just be a sec..."

"If you don't leave right now, I'm going to kick the living shit out of you."

Now Leah was getting scared. As the man yelled at her dad, he was too bright to look at directly; she recoiled and glanced away. She noticed her mom was fixated at the glowing man. Her dad, however, did not seem to notice the man's gleaming body. Leah, slowly got up with her free hand bracing her eyes from the bright lighted man, and started to walk towards her parents.

"Listen. My daughter and wife are here and you have no right..."

"I hope you get heart attack and die you bastard!"

Leah stopped and looked to the ground, clutching her eyes. The man was now indistinguishable and looked like a big ball of burning white light. After a brief moment, a hand gently touched her shoulder. She looked up, nervously, and saw her mother.

"You ok Leah?"

"Umm, I think so. Where's dad?"

"I'm here baby. Everything's fine. Let's just get out of this area."

Her mom and dad were on both sides of her as they walked away from the bad man and wonderful ice cream shop. Leah was dazed and quiet.

"Leah, did you hear all that?"

She continued walking but answered her dad. "Yea."

"I'm sorry sweety. Not everyone is very nice"

Leah nodded.

"Let me put that ice cream in the garbage and I'll grab a new one for you soon."

Without hesitation, she passed the half melted cone to her dad and he walked slowly to the garbage nearby. As he walked away, Leah's mom turned to Leah.

"Sweety?"

"Yea mom?"

"You were covering your eyes?"

"Yea."

"Why?"

"Because mommy, the man was shouting."

"Oh, ok." Leah noticed her mom was almost relieved. But Leah continued.

"And he was so bright. It hurt my eyes."

Leah's mom stopped in her tacks and looked at her with a deep level of worry.

"Did you see that too mom?"

As her mom was nodded with slight apprehension, both were startled to hear people shouting nearby. They simultaneously turned towards the crowd and in mutual horror, saw their husband and father laying down on the ground, one hand holding the vanilla ice cream, and the other, his chest.

CHAPTER 2

The day began like any other, though Alex knew something was amiss.

His migraine was finally receding, and that was more than a welcome relief. The forecast called for sun, no clouds, and 110 degrees. This was unusually scorching, even for LA standards. It was just before one p.m., and Alex was thankful that at least now he could enjoy a bit of the day's brightness. He had been having these migraines weekly for a few years now, and sometimes it could ruin his entire day.

While Sundays were not always a welcome sight, as Monday's work week moodily awaited, on this day, Alex was especially buoyant. After his late Sunday morning jog, his old college friend Laura would be visiting him. He had not seen Laura in five *really* long years. When the migraine started at the end of Alex's run, his mood quickly dissipated into lackluster melancholy. Though he was feeling brighter with each passing moment, a part of him was bothered about this visit. Laura never visited. In fact, since college, Laura was mostly absent from his life.

Laura Coxworth was a Boston native. At twenty-seven, she was a stunning woman with long, straight, full blonde hair that shimmered. While her blue eyes were dark and intense, she had a wide and discerning smile. Men were slightly uncomfortably to be in her presence. She was also taller than most women, and that sometimes made other women feel uneasy. Alex found it curious that Laura never gave the impression she cared much about how she looked. In all the years he had known her, not once did he observe her painting her nails, looking at a small mirror, or fixing her makeup, things that he saw most women do.

He and Laura met in his second year of college. Alex left his native Los Angeles and decided to move away, not from the warmth of the West Coast but from the loneliness and bitter memories of his past. Boston College had provided him with a partial scholarship based on above-average grades and some extracurricular activities that, in Alex's mind, were completely overblown, but he was grateful, as it helped him get away. Nevertheless, living in Boston that first year was not the change he yearned for. The weather was inconsistent, and the people were tough to get to know. He was not so foolish as to think that it would be paradise, but he was also disappointed that he had not made any great connections. On the second day of his second year, Laura had shown up in his macroeconomics course, and his outlook immediately changed.

It was early September, and the weather was beginning to shift. Alex had settled into his seat with the class a few minutes underway. Laura entered the classroom while the professor rambled on about the syllabus. Alex had not seen her before and fixed his gaze upon her. Alex was near the back of the large, raised lecture room, high above the professor's podium. While there were many seats unoccupied, Alex privately wished that only the one next to him was available. Laura continued to walk up the stairs and sat next to Alex. He was delightfully surprised.

"Hi, I'm Laura," she said quietly and reached out to shake his hand.

Alex hesitated for a second. He cursed his sweaty hands, as he had so many times in the past. He reflexively tried to dry them beforehand, but they still felt like they were bleeding sweat profusely. He brought his right hand to Laura, and she shook it firmly. She gave no indication that she just clenched a wet rag of a hand. He liked her already.

"Hi Laura. I'm Alex." He tried not to stare too intently. She was beautiful and friendly. Alex was smitten.

"Did I miss anything? My run lasted a bit too long, and I had to come straight here without changing."

Alex finally noticed her perspiration and felt a slight relief about his moist handshake. "Nope. The prof is rambling about what to expect this year."

She nodded, took her pen and pad out from her backpack, and stared intently at the professor. During the next hour, Alex had barely retained anything from the professor's teachings. He was mesmerized by Laura. When class ended, Laura turned toward Alex and said, "Up for a coffee?"

Alex nodded eagerly, knowing full well he would miss his next class.

On their way to the coffee shop that was located a few hundred yards from their class, Laura asked, "I don't detect a Boston accent. Where are you from?"

"I moved here from LA last year. For school. And I don't hear any accent from you. Where are you from?"

"I was born and raised in Massachusetts. Near here. But we did move around quite a bit."

They had ordered and received their coffees and sat in the corner of the shop. Several times, Alex had to look away from Laura, as he felt he was staring too much. Laura did not seem intimidated or bothered by Alex, and in fact she rarely moved her gaze from him. Alex was sure, though, that Laura was not motivated by attraction. He was generally comfortable and confident in himself but realistically viewed himself as an average-looking man. Over six feet tall, slim but solid build, thick brown hair, and hazel eyes, he attracted a sufficient number and type of women in his first year of college. But he knew that Laura was completely out of his league, and that was okay.

"So, where else did you live?" Alex asked.

"Well, we moved to Dallas when I was around twelve, then to Seattle when I was fifteen."

"Yuck. That must have been hard."

"Yeah, kind of. But ... yeah ... I guess it was rough at times."

"Yeah, I'm sure it was. Leaving your friends, school, your life ... I think anyone would find that challenging."

"Well, yeah. Kind of."

"You probably had a lot of friends."

"Not really. It was hard to keep them, and I like people, but not that much."

Alex smiled at Laura's comment but noticed she was looking slightly uncomfortable. He quickly changed the focus to himself.

"I didn't move at all until last year, and all I ever wanted was to get away."

Laura's complexion changed, and Alex was glad he was deflecting the attention away from her.

He continued. "I grew up in a suburb of LA, and it was just not fun. For as long as I can remember, I wanted to move. Get away. Just not be there. I always felt that way."

"And you never moved?"

"Nope. Never. Born, raised, and lived in Newport Beach until I moved here a year ago."

"Damn, that's a great spot. That must have been fun!"

"Nope. Not as much fun when you live there every day."

Laura looked inquisitively at Alex.

"It was okay. Don't get me wrong. But I don't surf, and I'm not a beach guy so, yeah, it was just ... all right."

Laura nodded and said, "I get it. Dallas was warm, all the time. And that's better than Boston's cold and Seattle's rain, but it did get overwhelming after a while. I guess even paradise can get stale if you're there too long."

Alex nodded in agreement - Boston was indeed getting stale but suddenly felt a little more fresh.

"Interesting. So, you said you always felt like leaving. Do you still want to get away?

From here? From Boston?" Laura asked.

Alex looked up at the ceiling in the coffee shop and after a moment, responded, "Huh. Well. No. I don't think so. Not yet, anyway."

Laura took a sip of her coffee, and Alex wondered if she could see that it was a half lie.

He had been feeling the urge to leave Boston growing over the past few months, but the inability to figure out where else to go prohibited Alex from leaving. Now, at this point, with Laura sitting across from him, he was not feeling that urge. He realized he was being reticent to himself. Largely because it was foolhardy to think that barely a couple hours with this person would change his mind so easily. Despite his internal motivational ambiguity, Alex was feeling better than he had in a long time. *This is nice.*

Wired from two large coffees each, Alex and Laura left the coffee shop smiling as new friends and made plans to meet again after. Over that fall semester, they created a weekly routine of coffee after class. Alex was finally feeling more comfortable and always eagerly anticipated conversations with Laura. Their conversations were always interesting, different, and relaxed. Laura was bright, energetic, and tough, but Alex felt at the time that she had some apprehension in certain conversations. Especially those about her parents and childhood. Alex never pushed hard, and he felt she understood; he too was holding back his childhood and parental issues.

One day in mid-November, a couple of months after they met, sat at the same coffee shop, the nature and complexity of their relationship altered forever. Laura had been quiet for the first twenty minutes while Alex rambled on about how he was uncertain if he was learning anything in business school. It was small talk that Alex hated, but Laura seemed to be carrying a heavy load on this day. Careful not be intrusive, Alex asked, "Are you okay today?"

"I'm sorry. I'm a bit off."

"No worries. Do you want to leave? We can catch up later."

Laura sipped her coffee with both hands to warm them. When they had walked to the shop together, it looked much warmer than it was. Novembers in Boston could be bitter cold, and this day proved one of them.

"No, I'm okay. I'm just cold and cantankerous."

Alex almost spit out his coffee. He looked up at Laura and asked, "What did you just say? Cantankerous?"

Laura smiled but only slightly.

"What are you? An old lady? Are you going to start yelling 'get off my lawn'?"

Laura giggled, and Alex smiled brightly. He was happy to see her in a more uplifting mood.

"Anything I can help you with? Do you want to talk? Do you want me to shut up?"

Laura took a deep breath, and her eyes became narrow. She looked around as if she were making sure no one was listening to them. Alex was feeling both intrigued and unnerved.

"Can I trust you?"

Alex was not expecting that but welcomed it nonetheless. He nodded and said, "Of course. I know we don't know each other that well, but I consider you my best East Coast friend."

"Well, yeah, Alex. I'm your only East Coast friend."

"Like you have anyone here either!"

Laura smirked but her expression hardened, as she continued. "I'm going to tell you something that you're probably not going to believe. Actually, you're *not* going to believe it."

Alex nodded and was about to agree verbally.

"Before you say anything or respond, just listen first, okay?" Laura asked with a hint of sadness and hopefulness. It was something vulnerable in Laura that Alex had not seen before. In all their previous conversations, she had been positive, inquisitive, and generally very upbeat, but today was different. Alex always liked deep conversations; it made him feel more alive. Though he was uncertain where this was going, he was eager to explore something more serious with Laura. Laura had not spoken for a few moments, so Alex asked, "Of course, Laura. Should I be afraid?" half-jokingly.

Laura seemingly ignored his question and continued, "Ever since I was a kid, I always believed I could sense things that others couldn't."

Alex nodded in affirmation; he felt quite similar. Being a high-level introvert, he had always sensed how others were feeling often long before they knew it themselves.

"Not for everyone. Just a few people. A few *types* of people."

Alex didn't understand where Laura was going with this but he listened intently all the same.

"Back when I was ten years old, my dad and mom had a rare but pretty big argument. My dad had some issues with his family at the time. His nieces, who were close to his age, were creating some havoc within the family. Both tried to institutionalize their mother, Dad's sister. Joanne, the older one, was the main instigator, while her sister happily went along with it. They believed their mom was developing dementia. Dad said it was bullshit. He was devastated that his sister was being stripped of her dignity. I don't think I've ever seen him so mad."

Alex could see Laura's demeanor quickly turn sober, as if she were recollecting something of grave seriousness. He was simultaneously fascinated and edgy. He wanted her to get to the point, not because he was impatient, but because of the heat rising slowly in his body.

"My mom was, is, always more level-headed than my dad. She tried to gently calm Dad down with a rational explanation, but he was having none of it. What happened next scared me and, well, changed my life forever."

At that point, Alex was dreading the part to be revealed. He had experienced a gut-wrenching amount of angst in his childhood and thought a well-known pattern was about to occur. He was wrong.

She continued, "As Mom tried to calm him and he got even madder, he finally screamed out, 'I hope Joanne gets hit by a car!'"

Laura stopped and was now on the verge of tears. Alex wanted to take her hand, but she was solidly holding the cup of coffee with both, and she held on for dear life.

"Wow. Okay." Alex was not wowed at all but relieved. He expected much worse and assumed this was simply run-of-the-mill family drama. He exhaled a sigh.

"Alex, that's not it."

Alex looked at Laura bemused, nodded, and remained silent.

"Even at ten years old, those words didn't bother me ... too much. I knew my aunt was probably a shitty person. But ... but ... it wasn't just the words."

Alex was confused. Patiently awaiting Laura's revelation. *What did she mean, it wasn't just the words?*

Laura looked like she had a tsunami of details to share, but Alex could feel she was holding back.

"What I saw froze me in my seat. I couldn't move. I couldn't talk. I ... I didn't understand it. But I knew. I mean, I *knew* it was bad."

Alex contemplated that situation and thought that he might not have reacted entirely differently. He wondered privately why this was such a big event in Laura's life.

"My mom left the room, and Dad went outside. I stayed frozen for what seemed like an hour, but it was only a few minutes. But I sensed something fiercely. When Dad spoke those words, he ..." Laura stopped midsentence, took a sip of coffee, looked at Alex, and then back down at her coffee. She sighed. Before Alex spoke, she continued.

"When he said those words, I knew something was wrong. Something bad was going to happen. I just knew it."

Alex was getting squirmy; he had so many questions. But he kept quiet, listening intently.

"I just knew that something bad would happen to my aunt."

Alex was arriving at this conclusion for some time and felt a sense of relief. He surmised something probably happened to her aunt, and Laura's guilt had gotten the best of her, even after all these years. He had the urge to show her his understanding.

"Ahh, I see ..." Alex tried to talk, but Laura was not done and interrupted him.

"We got a call the next day, saying Joanne got in an accident. She was driving to the food market when she lost control and hit a tree. She wasn't driving fast, maybe thirty miles per hour. She died at the scene."

Laura stopped talking and wiped her eyes gently. Alex felt empathy for Laura but was glad that she could trust him with her vulnerability.

He waited for a few moments and said, "Damn. That's really shitty. I'm sorry that happened."

Laura's gaze turned even more serious.

"Yeah, Alex, it sucked. But that's just the beginning."

Alex's befuddled expression wasn't meant for her to see, but Laura seemed unaffected by it.

"What happened to my dad. What he did. What happened afterwards. I've seen it play out several times."

Alex was intrigued.

"What do you mean ... several times?"

"Alex, if we're going to continue with this, we're going to need real drinks!"

CHAPTER 3

Laura was arriving today, and despite the residue of his headache, Alex was excited. His phone showed it was nearly three p.m., and Laura would be there at five. Despite Alex's insistence on picking her up at the airport, she was adamant about not bothering him. Though it was a Sunday, the traffic was still inconsistent, so he wasn't sure when she would get there. He was, nonetheless, excited to finally see her again.

As the coffeepot brewed a strong batch, Alex thought back to that life-altering conversation at the coffee shop with Laura. He recalled, almost embarrassingly now, how he surmised that Laura might not be particularly sane. He did realize that, even now, the things she said and was exposed to were other-worldly. But as that influential meeting pressed on, his viewpoint would slowly change.

*

"Let's go grab that drink. The rest of this gets harder and weirder."

The pub was a small, picturesque first-generation family-owned Irish bar in the heart of Boston, blocks away from campus. Laura had told Alex about the watering hole a while back; she had befriended the owners' son and became a semi-regular. Alex and Laura were not yet twenty, and while he was hesitant to go, she had been persistent. In Ireland and most parts of the world, she told him, eighteen was the legal age; they were old in relative terms.

As they walked in the cold November chill, Laura held on to Alex's hand. Alex knew it was not a romantic gesture. He believed that in him, she had finally found a confidant, a brother in arms; someone who was part of her small, inner world that she kept so discreet for so long.

"My childhood was so normal in so many ways."

Alex nodded.

"My mother is such a wonderful person. She's smart, warm, caring, and strong."

"I see the apple has not fallen far from the tree."

Laura smiled wistfully.

"Well, maybe not so much. But she's awesome. She homeschooled me a fair bit, which I thought was wonderful, especially as I got older."

Alex felt there was good reason for that.

"Dad was ... is, a driven man. He always has ideas and thoughts about doing things differently. He worked hard and traveled for work a lot. As I got older, and especially after a few of his episodes, he was gone even more."

"Wait? A *few* episodes?"

"Yep."

"Do you think he knew what was going on?" Alex did not actually believe it, but he needed to ask the questions.

"I'll get to it. And no, I don't think he knew."

Alex had so, so many questions.

"So, when I told you earlier about Dad and his niece, that was not the first time I actually saw this happen. It happened when I was seven, but I only remembered it afterwards. I guess the shock of my aunt dying, and what dad said helped me remember."

Alex remained patient.

"I remember the first time like it was only yesterday, even though it well over 10 years ago. Much like the Joanne incident, Dad was venting to Mom about his coworker. And again, he got angry and blurted out that he hoped that asshole crashes on one of his road sales trips."

Laura's grip tightened around Alex's hand. He could sense something different.

"So, when I told you earlier that it was just not his *words* ..."

Laura stopped talking, let go of Alex's hand, but continued toward the pub. Alex was slightly confused about where she was going with this yet enthralled by the conversation. He really liked Laura and thought she was bright, but the dialogue had made him question Laura's stability and the thought that his relationship with her might be temporary, and that was disheartening. He nevertheless pushed through with cautious optimism.

"What do you mean by that? What else happened?"

"Well, like what happened with Joanne, when Dad was really mad and just before he made the threat, my vision got really odd. I experienced the same thing both times."

Laura paused. They were a few minutes away from the pub. The day was getting colder, and the daylight was fading. Alex looked at Laura and felt pain for doubting her. He swallowed hard and bit down to subdue his skepticism.

"Both times, light started to emanate quickly from Dad. He literally started to glow – I was nearly blinded by it just before he uttered his wish against both Joanne and his coworker."

Alex was not a psychotherapist, but he presumed that this was explainable in psychological terms.

"Wow. That is a bit scary. What happened to your dad's coworker?"

"Well, I didn't even think about that event until I was ten. After Joanne died. That's when I remember what happened. But I did not know if anything bad happened then. So, I asked my mother about Dad's coworker. Mom at first didn't know who I was talking about. I had to remind her about the one Dad hated and was always angry toward. Then Mom's face went white."

"Do you think she realized then what was happening?"

"No, but I do think Mom thought Dad was sometimes a bad-luck charm. But I don't think she had a clue what was really going on."

"So, did she remember what happened to the cow-orker?"

"Yep, she did." Laura swallowed hard.

"And?"

"He died the next day. He got hit by a car walking getting the mail from his mailbox in front of his house."

"Jesus, that's horrible."

Laura nodded - it was horrible. Alex could see the pain in Laura's eyes. He continued to have even more doubt but felt sad for Laura and her family.

"So, after your aunt, no one felt odd or felt like this was strange?"

"No. I think I was the only one that felt like this was real. And of course, I didn't say anything."

*

Alex's memory rushed back to him while showering and getting dressed. He was delighted at his recollection of his time with Laura. He supposed it left an indelible mark on his psyche. He had thirty minutes before Laura would get there. His thoughts quickly went back to that memorable discussion with Laura nearly ten years ago.

*

After much talking, Laura finally relented and asked Alex what he was thinking. Alex could see that this was not easy for her. He was confused, doubtful, sad, and a little annoyed. He thought to himself that it was just all coincidence and that Laura was rationalizing these episodes; that she was trying to make sense of what happened and attributing a reason for the deaths she felt guilty about. Alex was doing his own rationalizing. Her dad basically threw out negative things into the world, and they happened; *okay, possible but highly unlikely.* Alex knew coincidence was the real culprit here, and Laura was just not accepting the obvious. But while the machinations of thought were turning in his head, he did not want to alienate Laura. He wanted to keep her as a friend, make her feel better, and not ruin this friendship, even if it were strange. He had to tread carefully.

"Well, that's a lot to take in," Alex said, careful not to sound insensitive. "That's a lot for a young girl to go through."

Laura nodded but looked apprehensive. Alex knew she could tell he was doubting her. They were moments away from entering the pub.

"Whether or not it happened for the reason you think, it's got to be tough to have gone through that." Alex had gone exactly where he did not want to. Once the words left his lips, he knew it implied he thought she was full of shit. He expected Laura to turn around, walk away, and never speak to him again, but she didn't.

"Alex, it *was* a lot. And I know you find it difficult to understand and believe what I'm saying. But you will. At some point, you will. Just try and keep an open mind." Laura's steely resolve was coming back, though he felt she might have real doubt about having Alex as a confidant. He did not blame her for this likely feeling, as he doubted it as well. Alex decided that he needed to be honest with her.

"Laura, I'm sorry. I'd be lying to say I didn't think this was all coincidence, but what do I know? If you're still up for it, I'm here, and I'll keep my mind open."

Alex was relieved when Laura grabbed his hand and entered the pub. As they nestled into a booth in the back corner, Laura ensured she faced the entire pub. Alex presumed she was cautious of others hearing her revelations, and he thought that was a solid decision. While Alex was experiencing significant skepticism, he was still riveted by the conversation and was anticipating Laura's bombshells. He also hoped that there was something he could be even marginally convinced about.

After they ordered their beers, Laura continued with the subject of her dad.

"After the family incident, I began to see Dad differently. Whenever he was really fired up and emotional about something, I could see him slowly start to glow. I realized that whenever Dad started to get angry beforehand, I would get uncomfortable and just leave. But, eventually, I didn't leave. I stayed and looked at him, to see what would happen, I guess.

"So ... what do you mean by glowing?" Alex wondered.

"Light would emanate from his body. What's the best way to describe it?"

"Was it like a bulb turned on?

"No. Maybe a slowly raised bulb with a dimmer. Basically, it was like a bright light slowly coming from the pores of his body. Getting brighter as he got more upset. And almost blinding when he made the threats."

Threats. Alex was fascinated by this part. He thought he earned the right to ask, "So, he says something bad, and it comes true?"

"Well, no."

"I mean, if he's mad enough or in a certain heightened and angry type state, something he says could hurt someone?"

"Yes, right."

"Could he see the light?"

"No, not that I know of."

"Your mom, could she see it?"

"No, she never reacted to or ever mentioned it to him or me. So, no, I don't think so."

Alex was perplexed. He still doubted the reality of Laura's story, but she believed it, and that he was certain of.

"So, this is a dumb question—if he was really happy, could he wish good things to happen?"

Laura smiled weakly. It was something she thought of often. "No, I only saw it when he was angry."

"And did it ever happen again ... I mean, did he ever hurt anyone again?"

Laura's complexion changed slightly. "I never saw it. I saw him glow up many times, but I quickly learned how to defuse his anger. I tried everything and got really good at deflecting his attention. Sometimes I was a little shit, but I had to help him, even though he had no clue what was going on. "You know the interesting part? When I turned fourteen, or around that time, I never saw him glow again. So, I don't know if he lost that part of him, but I certainly hope he did."

"Do you think it's all coincidence?"

Laura briefly peered through Alex and then looked away, not in disgust but in thought. Alex knew that he had to be open and honest, but it did not feel comfortable being so direct.

When their two pints of beer arrived, Laura took a hearty sip. Alex never saw Laura drunk but thought, *if there ever was a day ...*

"I wanted to ask you about this glowing. I know they glow, but why? And how? And why do you see it? And do you know others that see it?"

"I have very little idea, about any of it. I have theories."

"What are they?"

"Just theories."

"I know, but tell me what they are." *Even crazy girls can be cute*, Alex thought, then dismissed the thought with a hint of guilt.

"I think people glow when they're extremely angry. When they internally feel overwhelmed or excited or pissed off."

"But people feel like that all the time!"

"I know, but some people are different. Why they are different, I don't know."

"So, how do you see them glow? Not to be a dick, but why are you able to see it but not me?"

"I really don't know. Something in me sees this, and people like you just can't. I can't explain it. I know a few that glow and a few like me that can see."

Alex was both vexed and captivated. So much speculation but from someone so believable.

"After I saw dad glow the second time when I was ten, it took a few years, but I began to see more glowers."

Alex ordered two new pints and nestled in to hear more.

*

Laura sat across from Alex, sipping her beer, wondering if she had made a mistake. Over the past couple of weeks, she began to feel that Alex was a good, caring, smart person who could handle what she was sharing. She had never told anyone of this strange part of her life, other than her boyfriend Paul. She also never told Alex about Paul, but she had her reasons that she would share with Alex. *If* he stayed and heard her out, and didn't run away petrified. She was half expecting he would jump up and run out of the bar at any moment. Her mind wandered briefly to the time she saw another glower for the first time.

At age fifteen, her parents had moved once again, this time to Seattle. While she did not have much say in the decision, she would not have put up any fight. During the past year, her father became more solemn and quiet. His latest sales job in Dallas had ended unceremoniously, but strangely he was not upset about it, and that was more than fine for Laura. Her mom and dad did not make it a production, and after a few months found opportunities they were apparently excited about and moved the family to the Northwest.

The high school Laura entered was not all that different than Dallas. Just a bunch of kids with kid problems. Nothing out of the ordinary for most, except of course for her.

"In Seattle, in the early days of my new school, I was sitting alone at the back of the cafeteria for lunch. Of course, I didn't have any friends. It had been five years since I saw Dad glow, so I was starting to think this might be all in my mind."

Alex nodded a bit too agreeably, and Laura knew exactly what he was thinking. But on this day, she had come too far. Even at the risk of losing Alex as a friend, she could feel a load lift from her shoulders. She needed to disclose her experiences even if it was not to be believed. Even if Alex thought she was bat-shit crazy.

"These two girls began arguing, which quickly escalated to shouting. My first reaction wasn't 'oh crap.' By then, I almost forgot about the glowing. I was just annoyed that this was happening and almost didn't bother to look up. But I did."

Alex looked at Laura with anticipation.

"When I looked up, I saw a glower."

"That's what you call the people who glow?"

"Well, what else, I suppose?" She saw that Alex was interested but certainly not convinced.

"So, what happened?"

"I panicked. I got up and just about ran out of the cafeteria."

"You didn't try to stop it?"

Laura could see Alex regret this as soon as he said it. It was something she had scrutinized many times.

"Well, to be honest, like you're probably feeling right now, I don't know how much I believed this was real. Part of me thought I might have been crazy … insane … seeing things."

Alex nodded in affirmation. She could see the doubt in his eyes, but she didn't blame him.

"So, what happened?"

"As I was passing by them, trying to get away, I heard the glower shout, 'I hope you break your neck, you dumb cheerleader.'"

Alex remained quiet, and Laura was thankful. She could feel her heart beating out of her chest as she relived that day.

"So, obviously something bad happened, right?"

For someone who apparently was a nonbeliever, Laura was slightly bewildered at Alex's interest in her and the story. She reckoned that she made the right decision to disclose her life story to this person. At the very least, he would understand her, and for now, that was okay. She continued.

"The next day, I did not want to go to school. I knew … I just knew something bad would happen. Ultimately, I didn't have to go. It was all over the local news. A cheerleader named Jessica had an accident the evening before. During cheerleading practice, this girl was working on the backflip toss. It ended in disaster as she landed on her head and, well, you can guess what happened."

"She died?"

"No. She lived but was paralyzed from the neck down."

*

Alex was beguiled with Laura's story. While he didn't genuinely consider this to be real, the resolute belief, assurance, and lucidity with which Laura presented it held a captivating intrigue for him. He wondered if the beers were inhibiting his rational mind; nonetheless, he was more open-minded than just an hour ago. He was also staring into Laura's eyes, but she seemed not to notice or mind. He was mesmerized by her and her words. He was deep in evaluating and understanding who this person was.

As she began to retell the Seattle school story, Alex felt strange. He felt sadness, anger, and confusion, all while knowing that something bad was going to happen, which he knew would be a major factor in Laura's life. As Laura ended with the cheerleader's fate, he did not move. He could not move. Without warning, he felt like he was burning inside. His skin was itchy, and he felt like ripping all of clothes off for relief. Alex was dumbfounded and thought maybe he was having a stroke, while also realizing Laura's ability could, in fact, be real.

Strangely, despite his body and mind not being his own, what he thought of Laura surprised him and scared him even more. Could Laura be the reason all this was happening? Was she bringing bad luck to these people? Why was he thinking this? *Jesus Christ.* What was happening?

Laura grabbed Alex's hand, and what she said next scared the living shit out of him.

"Alex, you're glowing!"

CHAPTER 4

Alex Connor had a relatively normal and, in his mind, typically shitty childhood. He often described it to others that way. He realized as he got older and heard people's stories of growing up that more people than not had tough upbringings - varying degrees, of course, but crappy nonetheless.

His dad passed away a few years ago. After a stroke left him blind in one eye nearly a decade ago, he finally succumbed to liver disease. The years of heavy drinking took their toll on his dad. Being second-generation Irish, Alex would cringe about how folks would glorify alcohol; it was all too real, normal, and destructive in his household. This took a toll on him and his mother, who died a few years ago of lung cancer from years of smoking. He supposed the incessant cigarette use was her small way of dealing with his dad's alcohol abuse.

Alex rarely talked about his family, and though he always wished he had siblings, he was thankful that they did not have to grow up in such a hostile environment. He never talked about his childhood, since he could remember very little before the age of ten. It always fascinated him why he was unable, especially after so many stories of friends talking about theirs. He supposed it was traumatic and that is what happens to kids when they turn older. After the age of ten, well, he remembered way too much.

One such night lingered vividly in his adult nightmares. His mother and grandmother were in the bedroom, attending to his bedtime routine, while his father was out at the bars, engrossed in his drinking. Laughter and joy filled the air as the three of them reveled in each other's company, until a collective hush fell over them as his voice rang out, commanding, "Enough of that racket!"

Alex saw his mother freeze in her steps. While his grandma was old school and tough, at her advanced age, she would offer little resistance. His dad was not a physically abusive man, but the verbal diarrhea and alcoholic threats were enough to scare them all. The words from his dad rang in the air, and his mother and grandma stiffened up. He could sense their fear acutely, and it escalated further as his father forcefully ascended the stairs, his bullying demeanor intensifying. Alex could never recall much of what his dad said that day after his initial rant, but he did remember the shouting. He shouted Alex's mom's name, telling her that he wanted her out of that room. Alex stood by the closed door to his room. His petrified mother and grandmother were sitting on the bed holding each others hands. The bedroom door did not lock, and Alex's dad banged on the door, screaming, shouting, and cursing. Alex instinctively put his shoulder against the door and locked his right foot into the ground so that it would not open.

His dad was not a big man, but he had wiry strength. Nearly five foot ten and working in construction much of his life, he was lean, mean, and strong as a bull. This day, though, Alex felt scared but extraordinarily strong. As his father spewed profanities and banged on the door, he could not dislodge Alex. Alex realized years later that he was likely so drunk he likely could barely stand. But that day left an indelible mark on Alex's life. He remembered being very angry and very, very hot. His skin was almost burning.

*

"Alex, you're glowing!" After Alex heard the words, his mind raced back to that frightened and angry ten-year-old boy. He recalled vividly how he felt - how hot and itchy. Laura appeared frightened, causing Alex's thoughts to swiftly return to another distressing incident from his childhood.

When Alex was nearly fifteen, everything changed in his home life. Once again, his dad was on a start of a new bender. Alex had learned over the years that he could instantly tell when his father had been drinking, even if he had just one bottle of beer. It was his eyes. They just had that look. Alex had seen this in many people since and supposed he had become an expert at detecting alcoholism.

On this day, Alex was getting ready to go for a jog when he saw his dad and his souring mood - he was grateful to get out of the house. Before he left, though, he had to make sure that his father would leave his mother alone. His dad, when drinking, had a habit of being a complete shit to her, so Alex waited around to see how things would unfold. Unfortunately, it was more tumultuous than usual. His dad started to pinch his mother and tell her she was not pretty and that she should put makeup on to "brighten up." It was something he often did and it killed Alex to see how it bothered his mom. Alex stood in silence, feeling powerless, while his mother mirrored his stance, enduring the mistreatment.

Such occurrences were sadly routine and occurred with regularity. However, on that particular day, Alex's response diverged from his norm. He sensed a transformation within himself, a shift toward manhood, or at least the appearance of it. He was undergoing rapid growth, nearing six feet in height, and possessed remarkable swiftness despite not being heavily muscled. Alex had reached a point where people refrained from crossing him, with the exception, of course, being his father. As the verbal attacks and pinches continued, Alex's mom started to shake and sob. Alex had had enough.

"Dad, leave Mom alone!" Alex protested from across the kitchen.

His father, taken a bit by surprise, retorted, "What the hell did you just say?"

"You're hurting Mom, and she's crying, so leave her alone."

"You shut the fuck up, or you'll be next."

This type of insult and bullying was not new, but his father's face showed something that shook Alex. It seemed like genuine hate. In recollection, Alex always wondered why he did not run away or become paralyzed with fear. It was, in fact, the opposite. Alex filled with rage. He remembered that he was afraid of how he felt that day. The surge of emotions, particularly anger, was an unusual reaction for Alex, even in the face of these instances of bullying. But that day was different. He felt really hot as if something was burning inside.

His father started walking quickly toward him - Alex instinctively turned away toward the stairs. His father caught up to him when Alex was on the first few stairs and grabbed him by the bottom of his shirt and turned Alex around. That was when his dad punched Alex square in the stomach. It all happened in the blink of an eye, but to Alex, it felt like time stood still. Alex did not feel the punch. It did not hurt. What he felt, though, was his adrenaline exploding through every vein in his body.

Alex could hear his mother screaming for it all to stop. She was hysterical. Alex, to this day, remembered his dad's nefarious grin after the gut punch. After Alex raised his right leg and kicked his dad square in the face, his dad's demeanor quickly changed.

Alex's mom screamed in terror. Alex's dad recoiled and became utterly immobile. It was not from the kick; it was a glancing blow at best. Alex guessed that his dad probably never had anyone fight back. It was likely such a foreign thought to his father and he could not register it for a few moments.

Alex dashed down the stairs, breezing past his father, and into the kitchen where he seized a pair of meat scissors. Witnessing this, his mother's distress intensified. His father's eyes widened with fear, and as

Alex began to advance toward him, the father swiftly retreated in the opposite direction.

The event lasted less than a minute but felt like an eternity. And, it changed everything in Alex and his family's lives. If his mom did not stop him, he knew he might kill his father. When Alex finally relented, he glared at his dad and snorted, "If you ever do anything to mom ever again, I will kill you. If you ever touch me again, I will kill you. This is your first and last warning." Alex's memory of this was as fresh as the day it happened. It was a pivotal point in his life, dramatic and terrifying as it was. But in this moment, in this day, what Alex remembered most vividly was how angry and hot he felt. He felt like his insides were on fire.

As this memory flashed across Alex's mind, he felt Laura's hands wrap around his gently. He remember being hit what felt like a breath of cold air, though he barely could make out the words she spoke – something about glowing.

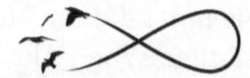

CHAPTER 5

With narrowed eyes, a slight headache, and an elevated heartbeat, Alex tried to focus on Laura. He shook his head in an attempt to calm himself.

"What ..." he said in a trembling voice. Alex now felt a pang of emotions enter his head: anger, sadness, and above all, guilt, for thinking that Laura was the cause of this. "What just happened?"

"Where did you just go?" Laura asked cautiously.

"Yeah ... I just ... I was thinking ..." Alex was still somewhat disoriented.

"Thinking about what? Why did you get so mad?" Laura wondered, still apprehensive.

Alex was still coming down from his emotional state but slowly returning to normal. "What do you mean, mad? I didn't say anything, did I?" Alex asked.

"No, thank God."

"But I was glowing?"

"Yes, really brightly. Just for a moment, but I was scared, Alex."

"Am I glowing now?"

"No, no, you're fine."

"Thank God."

Laura squeezed Alex's hand to comfort him. Alex was grateful, but he was not sure what just happened. This was happening a bit too fast for him, and Laura's nightmare story now had him square in the middle of it. He was not sure if he should get out of there and run away forever or stay and figure it out with Laura. For now, he would choose Laura.

"So, you mean to tell me you think I'm one of them?" Alex asked incredulously.

Laura paused, took a sip of her warm beer, and responded, "I think I've said too much. I think you were really upset just then, and I don't want that to happen again. Maybe I should just go."

Alex had always had a temper, but it was quite rare that it would be displayed outwardly. He could recollect only a few times when he got really upset. It took a lot to anger Alex, but when it did, he would feel it to his core. Now, Alex's anger was gone, but he certainly did not want Laura to leave.

"Laura, please don't go. I'm sorry. I'll tell you how I felt, so you ... we, can understand what I was thinking."

Thankfully for Alex, Laura let out a not-so-silent exhale, took another sip of her beer, and asked him, "So, where did you go when I was telling you the story?"

Alex relayed the entire history of those two personal events with his dad. Laura looked on without blinking an eye, only nodding and shaking her head. She did not speak or inquire until Alex was completely done.

"Wow, that is some sad stuff that happened to you."

"Well, it happens to more people than we realize." Alex grabbed his beer and downed a quarter of it before adding, "I don't know why I got so worked up. It triggered something in me, and I started to feel it again."

Laura sat quietly, obviously trying to come up with the next few words carefully. "You were glowing. Do you know what that means?"

Alex decided that a large gulp of beer was more important right now. He finished his glass. He did not really want to hear the rest but knew he had to, or else he would risk Laura sharing anything with him again. And if he was a glower, then did he unintentionally hurt anyone?

"Have I ever hurt anyone?" He looked at Laura but was asking himself.

Laura looked down at her beer and after a moment looked at Alex almost indignantly. "Do you believe in what I'm saying? About this ability I have, about what you have?"

Alex thought carefully before he answered. "I think so. It's all so strange and weird. I trust you, but this all is just screwed up and hard to believe it might be real. And if it really is, that, well, that's even worse."

Laura nodded. "I hear you. It is real, and you'll see someday. But I understand why you don't want it to be. It's a curse. To know these things and not be able to really help anyone."

"You just helped me!"

"True, but I couldn't always help my father. And what if I'm not around to help you when it happens again?"

Alex could feel the angst Laura was dealing with. He wanted to help her but treaded carefully. He was not sure if any of this was true, but to her it was, and that mattered. The way his body and mind just reacted to her story and his trip down memory lane did not feel normal.

"People do what they do. You can't be held responsible."

"Right. I know I can't control people, but wouldn't you want to know if you were inadvertently hurting people? I'm sure Dad would have wanted to know."

Alex nodded.

"So, you saw your father glow."

"A couple times."

"Right. And then you saw the cheerleaders."

"And then you, just now."

"Right. So, how many people *have* you seen?"

*

Laura wanted to run. When Alex started to glow, she wanted to get up, throw the beer in his face, and run for the door. She had not expected Alex to be a glower, and was not happy about it. She wanted to have a normal friend, someone who she could confide in, not someone *else* she had to worry about. But she had not run and instead decided that at least for a while, she would stay and see how this might all develop.

Alex was asking informative questions, but she could tell even now, he was essentially unmoved. What he just felt, that glow, could be construed as high blood pressure or just anxiousness. She knew differently and continued.

"How many people have I seen glow? That's a long story."

Laura's mind raced back to her the summer after she graduated Bellevue High School in Seattle. She was seventeen and eagerly anticipated the last year of school, not because she was excited about prom or the typical festivities bestowed upon seniors, but because she could get away from there after it was over. She needed to leave that school and frankly get away from her family; a nearly incessant urge to distance herself from her family - her father.

She had seen several glowing incidents after the cheerleader accident, but she avoided any confrontation with them and more importantly did not follow up on what might have happened. This avoidance stage at first was a welcome relief to Laura's anguish and guilt. The guilt was over her lack of ability to really help people. And she thought a lot about this. Guilt. She wondered why she had so much of it and felt it so deeply. People did bad shit all the time, and like glowers, many did it without realizing. Drunk drivers who were not bad people but thought it fine to drive while under the influence killed people too regularly. Parents ruining their kid's life but thinking they're wonderful role models. Hell, Laura thought, many world leaders killed innocent millions in wars for the sake of their own people. She tried to rationalize that her ability to sense when someone could hurt someone else was no different than observing inebriated people walking out of a bar and getting into their cars.

Except, deep down inside, she really did not believe this. If all the cases were good people who did wrong things, they *should have* known the difference. They were aware of their decision and knew that bad stuff could happen. The weekend warrior alcoholics who were too cheap to get a cab or Uber or simply too stubborn were not completely innocent. Going to jail if they were caught proved that what they did was inexcusable. The inadequate parents whose children bore lifelong emotional wounds could pose a challenging scenario. However, in the present era, being an uninformed parent was a deliberate choice. A simple online search about negative reinforcement would prompt even those lacking formal education to swiftly contemplate their parenting approach.

These folks could have helped themselves and avoided damaging others, but her glowing counterparts could not. They were not actually doing anything wrong but for saying unkind words, gossiping of sorts, and they had no idea the pain they were inflicting. And this, the act of not assisting those who lacked the awareness of their own distress, weighed upon her consistently—something she had borne in the past and continued to carry even more now.

That summer, she had convinced her family to visit a cousin in Alabama. Laura was eager to explore a little bit more of the country, and while Alabama was not her first choice, it was, after all, getting away. Her parents were reluctant, but surprisingly her dad convinced her mother, and so she set off for a week for Hoover, Alabama.

Her mom's sister was a nice lady who had that southern charm. Her uncle was quiet but funny, and their kids were all grown up and out of the house. Laura's mother found it odd that Laura expressed a desire to visit an older couple with whom they weren't particularly close. However, this choice felt ideal to Laura - a place of tranquility, peace, adorned with charming accents, and embraced by warm weather.

"So, Alabama, huh?" Alex was still here, asking questions. Laura was thankful.

"Yep. It was a nice little getaway until the game."

Alex looked on while sipping his beer. Laura noticed he went for a stronger IPA this time and thought that was a prudent idea.

During her visit to Alabama, she had decided she would go to her first ever football game. It had a been a quiet, pleasurable trip, but she was slightly bored, so she decided to go to the high school's Friday night game.

"A football game? Didn't realize you were a fan."

"Oh, I'm not. And especially after *that* game."

High school football in the Deep South was something she had read about many times. Entire towns would close down on Friday nights. It was a religion, and she was interested in seeing what the fuss was all about. She walked to the game, which was fascinating. They were of all ages -children, teenagers, moms and dads, grandmas and papas. It felt somewhat like a large cult, but of a jovial nature, and Laura had good vibes that this would be a fun experience.

"A good experience?" Alex laughed nervously, and Laura nodded knowingly.

To those that liked football, her seat would have been considered ideal. Positioned close to the fifty-yard line, offering a central vantage point encompassing the field and thousands of fans, all under the enchanting backdrop of an Alabama night. Even with Laura's limited knowledge of football, it was idyllic. Surrounded by her, the atmosphere resonated with laughter and smiles, accompanied by fans energetically waving oversized foam fingers and flags. The congregation of individuals clad in red jerseys metamorphosed the stadium into a crimson expanse, initiating a wave that rippled through the crowd following the national anthem. In her recollection, Laura experienced an unusual yet delightful feeling of fitting seamlessly into a vast, jubilant family.

"I can see that's not going to be the case." As Laura was recalling this pivotal moment in her life, she could see Alex was intimately interested in what she had to say. She had been thankful for his brief friendship and felt after this day, it would likely be a much longer one than she realized. Still, there was the fact that he was a glower. That was problematic. For now, she would not concern herself with it.

The Hoover football team was crushing a nearby local high school team, and the fans were jovial. She had planned to leave a few minutes early to avoid the crowd. Despite the evening having been enjoyable, she was growing bored and finding herself increasingly disinterested in the game.

"As I stood up to leave the game with a barely five minutes left to go, something caught my attention. On the field ... one of the players ..." Laura swallowed hard.

"A glower." Alex said it matter-of-factly.

Players and referees were trying to break up the on-field scuffle, making it tough for Laura to see who was actually glowing. After a few minutes, the referees managed to separate both teams, but the glower was left in the middle of the field. The player was glowing brightly. In the midst of the ruckus, Laura had subconsciously stood up and walked down the stadium stairs. Her instincts kicked in, unaware that there were thousands of people now leering at her. She had decided that she would try and distract the glower to prevent any harm to others. She descended to the lower section of the stands, and before security could intervene, she swiftly vaulted over the fence. Her heart raced, the sensation exacerbated by the glowing player who was vehemently shouting profanities. Laura wished she was not there anymore, but knew she had only moments to help this kid and whoever he might hurt. She could hear security guards scurrying behind her, and she ran as fast as she possibly could.

As she ran, she noticed the players and referees looking at her, all except for the glower. It felt like slow motion for Laura, and unfortunately, she had everyone's attention, except for the person she really wanted. He was still shouting at the referee and now bright as the sun; Laura thought he might soon burst into flames.

Finally, she could hear him clearly. He was screaming at the referee and now in Spanish. She was about start shouting herself before two security guards tackled her on the field. Her adrenaline still pumping, she landed face first into the field but managed to keep her gazed locked on the glower. His brightness immediately stopped as he stared directly into her eyes. She felt relief; she had saved him from disaster.

As the handcuffs were being placed on her hands behind her back, she felt as sense of pride. She had helped two people on this day, though no one would ever know it. But she did, and that felt good.

The glowing player, now without his helmet, maintained unbroken eye contact with Laura. His smile stretched wide, exuding an air of knowing. Laura's sense of achievement was abruptly shattered. A shiver traveled down her spine as the referees forcibly removed her from the field. She knew that the football player comprehended her ability to truly perceive his glowing. In that moment, someone other than Laura recognized her unique sight, and their own. Overwhelmed with fear, Laura was gripped by a sense of paralyzing dread.

CHAPTER 6

Alex could remember that evening at the bar like it was yesterday; it was etched in his memory forever. Laura's story about the glower at the football game still gave him a chill that ran down his spine. This was quickly replaced by anticipation as the as the doorbell rang. He got up from the kitchen chair and nearly ran through the living room to the door.

He paused for a second and peered through the small door window where he could see blonde hair flowing with the light breeze through his front door. The killer heat of the day was relenting, with a light wind and welcomed clouds. Laura was looking away from the door, still holding her small luggage. Alex felt sick, slightly disoriented though he was excited to see her, as it had been many years. He missed her so much. He had felt lonely since the last time he had seen and been with Laura, and yet strangely, he felt lonely at that moment. He swallowed hard and hoped that maybe she was truly back in his life, and opened the door.

Laura turned around with her beautiful blue eyes and beamed widely. She was still stunning; actually, more beautiful than the last time he saw her. The years had been good to her.

"Hey, you!" Alex said almost longingly and gave her a big hug. Laura held him tight, tighter than he ever felt before. They remained on the doorstep, quietly embracing for a few moments. Alex certainly did not want to let go of her, and he thought Laura felt the same.

"Are you going to let me in, or should I get a hotel?"

Alex chuckled, not wanting to let go, but relented and said, "Of course!" He picked up her luggage and led Laura into his place.

"How was the trip? Are you tired? Thirsty? Hungry? You need anything?"

Laura smiled and said, "Just one more hug, please."

She now had a tear running down her light, smooth chin. Her lips were quivering ever so slightly. Alex was thrilled to finally see Laura again, but something had gone wrong. Laura rarely got emotional in the years he had known her. He went to her and wrapped his arms around her waist, and while he had many questions to ask, he would wait for her to share when she was ready. When the embrace ended, Alex showed Laura to her bedroom. She asked him if she could take a shower and decompress after the long flight. He wished that he had known why she was here, and where she had come from; he really knew very little about her whereabouts for years. More pressing was her aura; Alex knew something was off.

As Laura ran the shower, Alex's thoughts once again went back to the conversation in that Boston bar many years ago, when Laura had told him about the glowing football player and his grinning, evil smile. Alex easily conjured up a perverse image in his mind's eye. He was beginning to feel anxious as the night long ago again came to the forefront of his thoughts.

*

"Holy shit, Laura, were you hurt?" The empty beer glasses were starting to edge out the small corner table, but Alex did not looked buzzed, nor did Laura feel anything other than angst.

"The security guards didn't hurt me. They were rough, but that was nothing compared to that guileful smile."

"Damn. So, what happened then?"

"The guards brought me back to their office, asked a few questions, and then let me go; especially once they realized how young I was."

"Jesus. At least you were safe. Did you go home to Seattle right after that?" Alex saw Laura breathe deep, taking another large sip of beer before she finally responded.

"The night didn't end there. Well. It kind of all started then."

Laura knew she had to tell Alex about Paul. Before this night of revelations at the pub, she was concerned because she wanted to have Alex as her friend, and he might want more; if she told him about Paul, he might just lose interest. However, knowing Alex was a glower, she was even more reticent about divulging that she had a boyfriend who could also see glowers. Now, it was risky. But she could not and would not withhold that information from Alex.

"So?" Alex asked impatiently.

Laura could see Alex was enthralled but also concerned. She liked Alex and was thankful she had met him; she continued with her story.

Once Laura left the now near-empty stadium, she had called a taxi on her cell phone and waited outside the stadium. It was nearing midnight, and Laura was spent; she'd thought first she would get a few hours' sleep, and she then head to the airport first thing in the morning. She was eager to leave and get home to the suddenly comforting thought of Seattle.

Thankfully, the cab came quickly; she was still shaken from the game, and while not frightened, she was not entirely comfortable being alone. She had texted her aunt and uncle, and they were aware of her whereabouts, but Laura insisted they stay in bed. The cab stopped, and the cab driver rolled down his window. He asked, "Laura?"

Laura nodded and then proceeded to open the door. The cab driver asked her one more question before she got in. "I'm driving my nephew to our home to stay tonight, if you don't mind. He's sitting in the front with me."

Laura didn't care, as long as she got to her aunt's place as fast as possible. She just wanted to get back to the room, pack, sleep, and then leave. The cab smelled of peppermint from a hanging air freshener on the mirror. It burned her nose a bit, but she was spent and was glad to close her eyes. It was a short drive and thankfully unadventurous. As she paid the cabbie and got out of the car, the front passenger door opened. Laura could not see the kid from the back seat, as he was wearing a hoodie. But when he got out of the car, he startled Laura a little as he asked quietly, "You are the one that ran onto the field tonight, right?"

For a second, Laura thought it might have been the glowing football player who knew more than he should. She was about to run for her aunt's door before the kid lowered his hood; it was not him. She felt relief and noticed his kind, curious, and handsome face. She exhaled; Laura reluctantly nodded and turned to leave.

"I'm Paul. I don't mean to bother you, but why did you go onto the field?"

A bit frustrated that she was being pestered by someone who could never start to imagine the things she's seen and been through, she raised her voice tersely and said, "Listen. I'm tired. I'm exhausted. And I just want to go to my room. Good night."

She took a few steps and grabbed her aunt's front door. Paul stood still and only spoke just before she entered. "You see them too, don't you?"

Laura stopped; unable to move and with her mind racing, she wondered if she had heard that question correctly. Finally, after what felt like an eternity, Laura turned around and asked, "What did you just say?"

"I know you're from out of town. And I know you're totally exhausted right now. If you want to talk, I'll be back here tomorrow morning at nine a.m. We can talk about the shiners then. Okay?"

Laura peered at Paul. Shiners? She felt like she was hit by a dump truck; she experienced a gripping fear that now there were two people who likely knew what she could see. But she also felt some sense of relief that she was not alone or crazy. Surprising herself, she answered, "Okay. Come by tomorrow at nine. If I'm still here, we'll talk."

Paul turned toward his uncle's cab and opened the passenger door. As Laura continued to stare, he turned his head and asked, "What's your name?"

"Laura." As soon as she said this, she regretted it. She had no idea who this guy was; he *seemed* harmless enough and apparently had secrets too, but this was foolhardy. She quickly turned and walked into the house.

Up in her room, lying exhausted on the bed, Laura pondered the night's event. For so many years, she felt very alone, isolated in a world where she avoided people for fear of what they could do and the regret she inevitably would feel. Before tonight, she had the option to run away from those people; her loneliness gradually becoming normal and even welcome. But the adventures of the football game in the godforsaken Alabama town changed everything. There were others like her, and even more like her father. She had hoped that it would all go away, but deep down inside, she knew that was not really an option.

But she also wondered if there existed a person who could stand by her, someone who could truly grasp the depths of her experience and empathize with the inner conflicts she was facing. Laura felt severe angst mixed in with some fleeting relief about this possibility. She was not sure if she would give Paul a chance tomorrow, but as she replayed the night, she fell fast asleep on the bed.

CHAPTER 7

When Laura walked out of the bedroom in Alex's condo, her hair dripped slightly unto her shoulder and then the floor. She had changed into more comfortable clothes—a white pair of jean shorts, a yellow sleeveless shirt, and flip-flops. Alex had to look away; sometimes he would stare a bit too long at Laura, and that was just not the nature of their relationship.

"How's life been treating you?" Laura asked, opening the fridge to get some lemonade. It was near seven p.m., and while the outside evening temperature was lowering, the air conditioning never seemed to get quite cool enough. Alex could see beads of sweat on her forehead and arms. She almost glowed—but not in the way he did. He thought a lot about *that* lately.

"Good. And you?"

Laura let out a barely perceptible sigh. Alex wondered if Laura was aware he was happy to have her there but very confused and disappointed that she had been AWOL for so many years. It was apparent to Alex that she had been avoiding him, for years. He was planning to have that conversation with her, but it was too premature.

Laura sat at the kitchen table with her legs folded beneath her and smiled uneasily. Alex felt Laura was partially somewhere else. She definitely was not herself, and he was eager to find out what was wrong.

"Remember Alabama?"

Alex nodded. *How in the hell could I not?*

*

Laura's brain quickly spun back nearly ten years to the night she met Paul. She went to sleep thinking that she'd wake up early and avoid him and go to the airport, straight back to her life in Seattle and forget all that happened in Alabama. It was, after all, the safest and smartest thing to do. When Laura woke up, though, almost against her own will, she decided to stick around. Her curiosity was getting the best of her, and she needed to hear what Paul had to say. She had hoped she would not come to regret this decision.

Paul had been at her aunt's place, standing alone on the curb with his hands in his pockets, head down and flicking at small pebbles along the sidewalk. She was looking out the window of her bedroom for a couple of minutes, debating leaving the house. She finally mustered up the energy and went downstairs and opened the front door. Paul turned around and waved at Laura.

"Hi, Laura. I'm glad you came out. I thought for sure you would not be here."

"I don't have a lot of time. I have a flight soon."

Paul smiled meekly and walked a few steps to the bottom of the stairs and sat on the last one. Laura sat with him and did not waste any time.

"What did you mean by *you see them too*?" Laura asked Paul, intrigued yet cautious.

"I was in the stands with my uncle, watching the game like you. I generally don't like to go to places with large crowds. Some might call that introversion, and while that might be true, as you know, it's not the main reason."

Laura nodded; she understood this all too well.

"I went to that game for a reason. I've known that shiner kid for many years."

Laura felt shivers run down her spine.

"I was actually there to see if he would do it again."

"Do *it* again?"

"Yeah. He has hurt several people."

"What do you mean *hurt several people*?" Laura was stunned. Her eyes were wide open, her mouth was hanging agape, and her right leg was shaking uncontrollably.

"Would you like me to stop?" Paul asked compassionately. He looked concerned. *Yes*, Laura wanted to say.

"No, please, continue. I'm fine."

"When he started to shine, I saw you jumping over the railing. I thought that was very strange; I mean, we see streakers from time to time or crazy people that run on the field, but young, attractive women, never."

Laura grinned weakly; she was not interested in anything beyond information. Paul continued.

"You weren't wearing any football fan gear and didn't seem to be a streaker."

Laura felt more angst about the conversation, but she did feel that Paul seemed like a genuine person. He was soft spoken, gentle but intense.

"You just stormed onto that field. You were running so fast. And then the security guards started chasing you. Everyone started to cheer you on."

Laura could not recall anyone cheering, but she knew she was focused on one thing and one thing only at that point.

"And then about ten yards away, when the shiner was near blinding me, and about to go off, you were tackled. By the way, how are you not hurt after that tackle?"

Laura was in fact, sore from that, but she pressed on.

"I'm much tougher than I look. Keep going."

Paul nodded. "And when you were tackled, Miguel just stopped shining, instantly."

"That's his name, Miguel?"

"I think you stopped him from hurting someone."

Laura let out a noticeable sigh. She had hoped that she could stop someone from getting hurt.

"Paul, can you tell me what you mean by shiners and how he hurts people?"

On the front porch step of her aunt's house, Laura sat entranced by Paul. Her initial fear was replaced by hope that someone else understood what she had been through and what burden she faced.

Paul had realized that he could see people only a couple years ago, and Miguel was Paul's first.

"Your first? That would be funny if we were talking about anything else other than this," Laura quipped.

Paul chuckled, and his face turned slightly red.

"Yeah, I guess I could have more enjoyable stories to tell, except I really don't."

Laura nodded. She knew that sentiment all too well.

Paul had first seen Miguel shine in Hoover High school a couple of years ago when Paul tried out of for the football team.

"No offense, Paul, but you don't really seem like a football player."

"I'm not. I tried, but yeah, I'm not."

Paul was not a small man, but even at fifteen, five-eleven with a skinny build, he looked more like a referee than a player. His real first encounter with Miguel, though, was not on the field but at a Saturday night football players party.

"A lot of the high school kids would go, get drunk, get stoned, make out, you know, what kids do."

"So, when did he shine?"

Paul was there for a couple of hours and did not drink, as his uncle would be picking him up early. He had an early curfew, so he was saying goodbye to some of his buddies. On his way out to the door to call his uncle, he heard someone shouting across the street. One person was speaking in Spanish.

"Miguel." Laura said matter-of-factly.

Paul nodded.

"That's when I saw it. I saw one of them."

"I call them Glowers."

"Works just as well as Shiners I guess." Paul looked at Laura and smiled.

"What happened then?" Laura could see that he was not apprehensive or internally torn. He was matter of fact and almost energized by this. She wondered if he felt the torment that she did about her *gift*.

"When the shining ... sorry, glowing, stopped, he let out a massive laugh. He laughed while he was walking away and got into his car and left. The other guy started to walk toward Paul back to the house."

"Did you ask him anything?"

"Yeah. I asked him if he was okay and what happened."

"And?"

"He said something like *that guy's a real dick.*"

"That's it?"

"No. He also said that Miguel wished he got hit in the head with a bat at his next baseball game."

"Oh shit." Laura's hair stood up on her arms, and she knew what was likely to be said next.

"Yep. Oh shit, all right. Two days later, this talented baseball player, Leroy was his name, was beaned in the head with a bat."

"Jesus."

"He was in a coma for five days. Permanent brain damage."

Laura looked at Paul and for the first time saw empathy. She had felt this way a few times in her short life, and now there was someone else with similar experiences. She could not help but feel a sense of belonging.

CHAPTER 8

Back at Alex's apartment, the night was beautiful and warm; he and Laura were sitting and relaxing on the small back deck, staring at the stars. A light breeze off the Pacific Ocean helped keep them cool and the wine warm. They were reminiscing about Alabama and how Laura first met Paul and learned about Miguel, and that was when she started to weep. Alex was taken aback; he had never heard Laura cry. This was the second time today that she was tearful, though this time it was nearly uncontrollable. Alex pushed his deck chair toward Laura and hugged her tightly. For a little while, she laid her head on his shoulder. He always felt that she possessed great strength and resilience, much more than him; but whatever had happened or was happening must be really bad, because, clearly, she was not in a good place.

After a short while, Laura retracted slightly from Alex, composed herself and said, "I don't know where he is. I haven't heard from him in a couple of weeks. And I'm scared he's ..."

Her voice trailed off, but Alex knew what she meant. He had met Paul only a couple of times during college, though Laura kept the meetings quite short. Alex had liked Paul; by most accounts, he seemed like a good guy. Through Laura's descriptions, Paul was good to and for her, though Alex was not sure how much he fully trusted Paul. He had never told Laura, but he believed Paul had hero syndrome—someone who really needed to make a difference and would or could put himself or those around him at risk. But fundamentally, Alex was unsure. He also knew deep down he was a bit jealous of the time Paul spent with Laura. The years apart from Laura never helped nor hindered Alex's belief in this matter.

"What happened, Laura?" Alex felt a heavy weight pulling him down.

*

Laura was frightened, but she did not imagine breaking down in front of Alex. Still, even through the embarrassment, she could not stop the tears flowing down her face. She was thankful that Alex was still supportive, even though she had not been a great friend to him over the years. But at this time, she was thankful that he was holding her close. As she sat outside on the deck on what should have been a beautiful, relaxing evening, fear and sadness poured out of her as her mind drifted to Paul.

After she met Paul on that fateful night in Hoover, Alabama, they became best friends and then eventually, lovers. The shared experiences of their young world bound them like no one or nothing else could. It was a long-distance relationship, but they talked for hours nearly every day for the first few years. Laura trusted Paul and knew that he adored her; they often talked about life, school, family, interests, but mostly about their ability to see glowers.

Early on in the relationship, the discussions were cathartic for both of them, as far as Laura could tell. But as time progressed, Paul grew weary of the conversations; a lot of talking but not a lot of action, he would say. He began to make plans, and at first, Laura was intrigued. Paul wanted to make a difference, and at first those plans were broad and idealistic; he wanted to help those who did not know they were hurting others. Eventually, Paul's interest became somewhat obsessive. Around that time, Laura had met Alex in Boston.

She had not told Alex about Paul until a year into their friendship. She could sense that Alex was hurt when she divulged the news, and she had expected that, but she had her reasons, and they were valid, at least in her mind. Paul was a senser who could see glowers, and Alex was a glower. Alex could potentially hurt anyone, and Paul would see Alex as a threat. So, she limited their physical interaction throughout the years; she had only allowed Paul and Alex to meet each other a couple times for a few minutes. She knew this was the only way she could protect them. What was worse though, she had also never told Paul about Alex's glowing ability. She now hoped she would get the chance to tell him.

*

"Laura?" Alex nudged her to continue. Their wine was low, so he poured them both a healthy amount.

The night was still beautiful, but he had brought out a blanket, and both of them laid it across their legs.

"So much has gone on since we finished college. Paul wants to be a hero, Alex; he always wanted that."

Alex wanted to blurt out *I knew it* but held it inside.

"He wanted ... *wants*, to stop the 'bad shiners,' as he calls them. He does not want them to hurt people."

Alex nodded. He was concerned about her use of the past tense; that seemed quite odd, he thought.

"He started before college ended. He had created a list of people that he knew or thought had this problem."

Immediately, Alex thought, *am I on it?*

As if Laura read his mind. "You're not on it. I never told him about you. Well, not about your glowing. And I only saw it once, Alex. But anyway, he doesn't know."

Alex felt both relief and pain. The relief came from the fact that only one person knew that he had it; *if he had it*. He still was not an absolute believer. But now he realized that Laura also feared how Alex might hurt someone—Paul and maybe her. Alex wondered if she was scared of him. He kept these feelings deep inside. There were more important, or at least, immediate matters at hand.

Paul had been an excellent student and had a job with an engineering firm in Atlanta. Laura had moved in with him after college. However, most of his free time was allocated to designing a plan to find and document all the glowers and sensers that Laura and he could locate.

"Sensers? You're using that now?"

Laura let out a little laugh. Alex had suggested the name "sensers" to Laura during one of their deep conversations during college. Apparently, it stuck, to his amusement.

"Initially, I was all in."

"Damn, Laura. That seems, well, idealistic, and a bit risky, don't you think?"

"It was that, but it was also a mission. Our mission. Something we could hold on to. And at first, it helped us with our anxiety."

"Anxiety?" Alex had a rough idea what she meant, but he had to ask. He had spent many years debating the substantiality of sensers and glowers. He wanted to explore the rationale for her feeling so guilty and wanting to help or save everyone. He knew most of it related to her father, but a lifelong mission? It seemed overkill in many ways.

"Yes. Anxiety."

"But why?"

"Why what?"

"What makes it your life's purpose?"

"It wasn't mine!" Laura sounded slightly exasperated.

"Listen, I get it that you and Paul have gone through some stuff, some horrific stuff. But it's not your fault. Lots of people do stupid shit. You can't change people. They are who they are."

"We've been through this before, Alex." Laura sat up straight and threw the blanket off her lap.

"I just want to know...what's this inner drive to protect people from this? It's so hard to even believe. Why fight a battle you can't really win? Even if it's real, how can you stop any of this?"

Laura looked disappointedly at Alex. He knew she had always believed he was on the fence, and that was okay. He was aware that tonight she needed him to listen, and he was doing a lot of talking. But he had to understand the *why* because he knew he was being dragged into the middle of their mission.

"Alex, I've seen my father do destructive things. Just because he's not aware of them doesn't make them any less real, or well, effing shitty."

"Right, but lots of people do bad stuff." He was adamant about truly understanding why Paul, and apparently Laura was now on this grandiose mission.

"He's my *dad*!"

"I get it, so why not just help your dad? Have you even tried to help your dad?"

Laura looked at Alex like she wanted to punch him in the nose. But he was right. Why didn't she at least try to help her dad? He believed she was ultimately afraid to, scared that her father would think she's crazy or ultimately disown her for thinking that he was, in essence, a murderer.

"I'm sorry. I know something has gone wrong for Paul, and I want to hear about it, but why this crusade?"

Laura took a deep breath. Alex had many of these types of conversations with her during college, and he felt it likely stopped them from having a closer relationship. Alex could get mad, and though he never ever glowed except for that one night at the pub, Laura was probably scared that he could hurt someone. Paul, her family, friends, and maybe even her. Alex felt like he was a good man, but he was a glower, and Laura believed glowers could not ultimately control themselves all the time.

"Alex, if you felt responsible for other people's deaths, especially those close to you, how do you think you would feel? Do you think you could just turn your brain off? And if you saw people glow and knew they were about to likely hurt or kill someone inadvertently, would you just lay idly by, letting them do it? Or would you try to do something about it?"

Alex nodded. "Yes, I would try to help those close to me. But, you could get *yourself* killed"

Laura shook her head. "So, imagine this: you see a parent glowing and angry at their child, but you don't know them. What would you do? Would just turn away and get on with life?"

Alex looked at Laura disapprovingly but she continued.

"It's not a passive problem. It's not like someone who drinks too much and drives. You don't really see that, and it's almost impossible to stop it. And frankly, you really can't do much with those type of people. But someone who's actively using something to hurt others, whether or not they know it, and you, and only you, have to power not only see it, but you, and only you, can help defuse it. Wouldn't you?" Laura seemed exasperated.

Alex looked away and pondered. He supposed if Laura was a glower, she would be as bright as the sun. He also realized she did have valid points.

"Okay, I get it. I'm sorry for probing and pushing; I just needed to understand the *why*. Can you continue? What has Paul gotten himself into?

"Oh, Alex, so much shit has happened. So much."

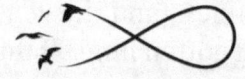

CHAPTER 9

On the back deck, Alex and Laura were buzzing from a second opened bottle of red wine. Laura was looking away from Alex, wondering, he assumed, how she would proceed.

"I have to tell you some of the things that happened, so we can try and figure out what could have gone wrong."

Alex nodded and asked, "Is Miguel involved?" The story of Miguel and Alabama had been imprinted in Alex's head. Laura had only told him the story once, but he could never escape the feeling that Miguel could somehow be part of the Laura's life again. Though he never said anything to Laura, he felt it nonetheless.

"No, it's not Miguel. At least I don't think so. Our intel on him is that nothing has changed."

Intel? Alex was not sure that Paul and Laura's fascination was simply that anymore.

"A couple months ago, Paul and I were in Huntsville for a rare weekend getaway. At a restaurant one evening, we saw a glower. A young woman. She was sat with another woman; friends, we assumed."

Alex was readying himself for another tragic story.

"But this time, it was strange, or I guess, stranger. The glower didn't seem angry or mad. She was just glowing. And the lady who sat with her was as cool as a cucumber. The casual onlooker would have noticed nothing. But the glower was as bright as the sun!"

"Hmmm." *Indeed*, Alex thought, *this is odd.*

"Then, before Paul and I could even try and defuse the situation that apparently didn't need defusing, she immediately stopped glowing. It was a big relief, but very strange."

Alex was trying to make sense of this and asked, "Were they like you and me? A glower and a senser?"

"Probably. Actually, it's very likely. Paul had talked to the waitress in an attempt to get their information, but of course, she would not give it. Though, she did tell Paul they were both regulars on Saturdays. So, we did the four-hour drive from Atlanta for three weekends in a row just to see if we could see them again."

"Damn. But if they seemed harmless, why?"

"Obviously, they know more about this than we do, so we needed to find out more."

Alex nodded. He was not so sure how obvious it was, but he stayed quiet to let her proceed.

"Finally, on the fourth weekend, we saw them again!"

Alex squirmed in his chair. While he was intrigued, the awareness of these gifts in others also meant there were more complexities; more opportunities for others to do the wrong thing. This was no longer a large secret between Laura and him.

"So, what happened?"

Laura took another sip of the wine. "Well, it didn't take long for us to learn more about them."

"How so?"

"As soon as we sat down at the restaurant, the non-glower lady walked straight to us."

Alex's heart was racing, anticipating the worst.

*

At the restaurant, Laura and Paul had sat down, tense with anticipation over finally locating the same two ladies. It had been a month, and they might have given up if this trip was not successful. In hindsight, Laura thought that might have been not so bad. A waitress took their coffee order, and just as she left the table, the non-glowing lady hovered above them at the table. She spoke before Laura and Paul could mutter a word.

"Hi, Paul and Laura. I know you are following me. You have been here for weeks. And I think I know why you are following me. But you should stop it immediately. You're both in way over your heads." She threw a business-type card down on the table and turned and walked calmly out of the diner with her glower friend behind her, looking away from Laura and Paul.

They both sat speechless and temporarily stunned, embarrassed that their undercover job proved remarkably inadequate. But mostly, they were bewildered by this lady's omnipotent air. And she knew their names? As their coffees arrived, the waitress didn't notice their complete silence and half-open mouths. With a sinking realization, they were indeed in over their heads.

*

Alex rose from the patio couch and headed into the condo to grab another bottle of red wine. Despite feeling slightly dizzy from drinking, fear of the unknown was the main cause of his unsteadiness. His hands trembled at the thought of the danger Laura and Paul were in. The situation had escalated from occasional accidents to a game of espionage, with the outcome uncertain. He steadied himself before walking back to Laura. He did not want to show her how terrified he was for her.

Back on the patio, Alex said, "Jesus, Laura, that's scary as hell. Who was actually spying on who?"

"I wouldn't call it spying, per se."

Alex looked at her with a skeptical expression; she was visibly annoyed but resigned.

"Okay, you're right. Whatever. The point is, they had probably noticed us the first time we saw them, and Paul and I were completely oblivious to it."

"And the card she gave to you guys? What was on it?"

"Just her initials, LJ, and a number. That was it."

"That's it?"

"Yep. It was strange."

Alex could tell Laura was also getting either too tired or too tipsy. But before they stopped, he had to get to what happened to Paul. "So, Paul? Where is he?"

*

Laura was driving the car home to Atlanta, white-knuckling the steering wheel, while Paul was looking at the card that they received from this mysterious woman. After the encounter with "LJ," Paul and Laura debated calling the number on the card. Laura was apprehensive; in fact, she was slightly terrified. This lady knew too much and was too aware; anyone with that power was bound to be dangerous or at least had the potential to put Paul and her in danger. Paul, on the other hand, was nearly euphoric. It was the break he was looking for and was adamant about calling her, sooner rather than later. The debate went on for nearly the entire trip back from Huntsville to Atlanta, though Paul's over-eagerness provided little room for Laura's concern; finally, against her good judgment, she acquiesced.

"Okay, Paul. You win, let's call her. But please, be careful."

Before her last word was fully out, Paul was already dialing the number, and the car's Bluetooth began to ring. Laura was nervous, and she could tell Paul was elated, and that made her even more edgy. After four rings, the ringing stopped, and there was silence for what seemed like an eternity. Paul finally asked, "Hello? LJ? Are you there?"

"Yes."

"Okay, good. This is Paul and Laura; the ones you met at the restaurant."

Laura thought that was rather an amusing description of the encounter. There was no meeting. No discussion. *They* were stalking LJ, yet she was apparently much more aware of them.

"Yes. I know much about you both. Hello, Laura and Paul."

A slight shiver ran down Laura's back. She wished Paul was driving; she was having a hard time concentrating, and her hands would be shivering if not for the tight grip on the cold plastic steering wheel. She briefly pondered stopping the car, as her hands were trembling and her mind racing. She glanced to her right and saw that Paul was grinning. Laura was simultaneously perturbed and perplexed about his demeanor. This is when she really began to doubt the relationship with Paul. They were lovers, confidants, cut from the same cloth and mission bound. The years with him were exciting and had a purpose, but he was starting to become reckless. Laura strongly felt that he was putting them both in undue risk.

Alex would never do this. Laura was surprised this thought popped suddenly in her mind. She supposed it was because Alex was very different than Paul. He was solid, consistent, listened, and considered consequences. Laura always thought Alex was her best friend, but she felt that she could not get closer to him because of his *ability*. And with Paul being somewhat of a wild card, she felt Alex would always be in danger. Naturally, revealing Alex's gift to Paul was out of the question. Her reasons were numerous, extending beyond the fundamental betrayal it would represent - a betrayal underscored by her wavering faith in Paul. As for Alex, she had, and would continue to, bury any thoughts about anything beyond a friendship. It was just too risky.

She also never told Paul her father's ability to glow. She started to use, or at least try the word *ability* recently, in part because there were good people who had it; some like Alex who never hurt anyone and others who would hurt those who hurt others. But mostly, she used it because Paul often called it a disease. While it was not that far from the truth, it bothered her immensely. Paul would no doubt put Alex and her father on "the list." The many binders and pages of people that Paul had written on, which she had helped build, was growing larger. But she believed he had more plans than just surveillance and research. She could sense this; while she could sense glowers visually, her belly screamed that something was just not quite right with Paul. And for that reason, she could not risk telling Paul about Alex.

"So, how do you know about us, LJ?" Paul asked, temporarily startling Laura, but he did not notice.

"Well, Paul, in some ways, probably the same way you know me."

Laura had seen lots of these types of people; those who tried to be mysterious, interesting, and liked to play riddles. She couldn't stand them.

"What do you mean by that?" Paul inquired.

"I've been searching for people like us for many, many years."

Paul and Laura glanced at each other, with Laura shaking her head and Paul grinning even wider. Laura was not expecting much from LJ. She was wrong.

*

Laura was surprised how open LJ was but was still very wary.

"I have the same gift as I'm assuming you both have." Laura and Paul both recoiled slightly at LJ's description. *Gift*. It felt much more like a curse, though Laura knew Paul was much more excited about having it.

"I realized at a very young age that I possessed it. It took me quite a long time to believe it was real and that I wasn't cursed," LJ continued.

"We both had similar experiences. How much do you know about this gift and about glowers?" Paul was insistent, eager to understand, and while Laura shot him a look of apprehension, she too was curious.

"Listen. I don't know your intentions. Both of you seem to be good people who are just trying to learn. You're obviously trying to figure shit out, so here's what I can tell you. Very few people have these gifts, sensing and glowing as you call them. They're really rare. No one, as far as I know, understands why."

"Is there a genetic reason?" Paul was fascinated. Laura was also intrigued but couldn't shake a sense of trouble emanating from LJ.

"We have not been able to correlate anything genetically with it. But there's still much work to be done. Most people we find out about who have the gift are those who post about it on the internet, and they're mostly sensers. That's who we usually first talk to. The glowers, mostly, are completely oblivious, and many can't ever come to grips with believing they possess the ability and have hurt people unwittingly."

Laura could sympathize with this, as her father would likely not respond well with the revelation that he was a glower. She hoped she never would have to engage him in that conversation.

"So, LJ, how does the glowing occur? What makes people glow, and can they do it for things other than hurting someone?" Paul wanted answers.

"From what we know, glowing only happens when someone is in a really negative state. Mostly though, that state is involuntary, though a few can achieve that state on demand. They're the ones that scare me the most."

Paul and Laura were nodding and turned toward each other and mouthed the word "Miguel." They weren't sure if he could really do it whenever he chose, but he was the only one they encountered who seemed like he was able to.

"And unfortunately, we've never seen anything good come from a glowing episode. And God knows we tried. Do you know many glowers?"

Laura froze in her seat. The words were reverberating loudly in her head, while Paul seemed entirely enchanted by the conversation. Laura's gut fired bolts of fear about LJ; keeping her father and Alex's glowing secret was more imperative than ever. LJ was involved in something, and Laura knew it was not on the straight and narrow. When LJ spoke *God knows we tried*, Laura's innards turned mercilessly.

"Yes, yes. We have seen several of them over the years." Laura punched Paul in the right arm and mouthed *shut up*. Paul looked surprised and waited for LJ to continue.

"Good. Us too. Most are harmless, or at least harmless in a way that they don't intend to hurt anyone."

"Who is *us*?" Laura could not wait any longer. She needed to know what LJ was really about.

"I am part a group that was formed long ago. A group to help folks like you and me. And especially glowers; we try to help them understand it and, of course, to control it."

Paul smiled, and Laura turned toward him; after seeing her reaction, he finally looked confused, though not for the reason she wanted. Laura quickly realized that she and Paul were on two completely different mental tracks about LJ. She was worried about this organization that LJ ran or was part of, but Paul was only excited to learn about. Alex and her dad flashed across her brain and the depressing thought that Paul most likely did not want the best for them, or at least their kind. She was feeling exhausted, confused, and angry with him. However, she knew this was not the place or time to confront her feelings to him about this. Instead, she asked, "LJ, who is this group you are talking about? And is it legitimate? Are you doing things you should not be doing?"

After a brief moment of silence, LJ responded, "That's enough for now. I'll be in touch with you soon." And then she hung up. Paul was beaming.

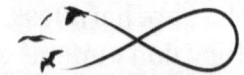

CHAPTER 10

"Can you believe there are others like us? We're not alone in this battle."

Paul's enthusiasm was bugging Laura, and she felt the urge to ask him to pull over to get away from him. She knew he was oblivious to the potential risks, or more worriedly, he did not care.

"Paul, does any of this make you uneasy? Aren't you concerned at all about her and whatever goddamn group she's part of?"

"If people are doing bad things to other people, we can't stand idly by. We have to do something about it."

"What the hell are you talking about? This crusade is about awareness; our awareness. Remember, we're trying to figure this out! To understand it better and maybe help *some* people. We can't help everyone!"

He stared out the windshield, squinting though there was no sunshine. Laura felt his pondering was over her lack of support - he was right to think that. She continued,

"I don't want to be part of what LJ is doing. She's acting like a god somehow."

"Wait, what?"

"Come on, Paul. Get your head out of your ass. She's been tracking people, recruiting people, testing people, deciding people's fate. Doesn't that feel like she's working a pretty shitty angle on all of this?"

"She's *doing* what we've been trying to do. She's just further along."

Laura finally stopped the car at a gas station. He looked at her with a mix of love and disappointment.

"We don't know what they're doing so let's not get ahead of ourselves. I'm sure they're not hurting people. And frankly, people like Miguel don't deserve to be left idle. Something needs to be done, and I think we just hit the motherlode for help. I'm excited, and you should be too!"

Laura was exasperated. She sat quietly, looking straight ahead and contemplated the past few years. It was apparent to her at that moment that she had traveled down the wrong path with Paul.

*

Back on Alex's patio, it was late evening, and Laura was bone tired. She had a strong buzz from the wine and had enough talking for one evening. She got up and said, "I'm really beat. Can we finish this tomorrow morning?"

Alex stood and put his arms around Laura's lower back, and hugged her. He did not say anything and did not easily let go. He lightly shook his head to himself, realizing the thought of anything with Laura would be taking advantage of a torn and drunk friend. He reluctantly let her go and followed her into the condo, watching her quietly walk into the bedroom and quietly close the door.

Alex sat on the couch and stared at the painting on the wall. It was a black-and-white canvas. While he'd had it for a long time, it still captivated him, though most of his friends who saw it thought it was slightly creepy. A straight, narrow road surrounded by large, but slightly barren trees diverged into two paths. The paths looked nearly identical, but one felt strangely inviting, and the other felt dangerous, with both leading into an enchanting and dense forest. He'd stared at this painting for many, many hours in the past, and he wasn't sure what the difference in the paths was, but he felt it. They both *looked* the same, but they sure felt different. He felt that he placed his life in front of this path, and that it was his internal compass of fear or hope that led him to view the roads differently. Of course, he felt this way much of his life. One road is presumably safe; that suggested a trail that leads to love, happiness, and wealth. The other was full of pitfalls and potential treachery. Of course, he long ago realized he did not choose either one, or at least he felt he had a foot on both paths. The treacherous path seemed more alive, but he avoided it frequently. That was the path of Laura. While he sat, slightly drunk and tired, he imagined Laura was deep inside the dense forest, waving to him to enter it. He quickly dozed off into a dream or nightmare, he wasn't sure which. Laura still standing, waving and waiting for him to make a choice to enter with her.

*

The next morning, Laura awoke to the smell of eggs and bacon, and though her brain was groggy, with a slight pulsating headache, she was famished. She got up and while still in her pajamas, went to the bathroom and cleaned up a bit. When she arrived in the kitchen, Alex was laying the food on the table.

"Hey, you. Good morning. Coffee?"

Recalling last night, Laura's heart rose and sank simultaneously. She had told Alex too much, way too much. Heck, she always told Alex too much. She came here for his help but wanted to protect him by *not* putting him in the firing line. She did anyway. She wanted to leave right then and there but knew she couldn't. She had no one else except Alex to help her.

"Or tomato juice? Does your head hurt as much as mine?" Alex smiled, and Laura relaxed a little. She looked at him and briefly longed for him to hold her. She shook her head and answered,

"Yes, that would be great. I need food, liquids, and some ibuprofen."

During breakfast, Alex and Laura sat quietly. She was not sure how he felt and again wondered if she went too far. Finally, Alex poured them a second large cup of coffee and said, "I know last night was tough. And I know you probably feel like maybe you divulged too much. But for what it's worth, I'm here for you. But I really need to know, why are you here? I mean, what happened to Paul?"

Laura fought the urge to cry. It took all the effort she could muster not to break down. It was a strange feeling for her, an overwhelming combination of sadness and happiness. She was so grateful to Alex for being by her side. But she also felt that he was headed, along with her, for something terrible.

Alex asked softly, "Are you okay?"

Laura finally shed a single tear, got up from the chair, and went to Alex. She sat on his lap and hugged him. Hard. Alex realized then that Laura must have felt more alone than he ever thought. He held her, and neither spoke for a few minutes. Finally, Laura went back to her chair and finally answered, "Paul is missing."

*

Alex nodded. He knew something bad happened, and Paul was seemingly unaware or uncaring about the risks.

Before Alex could speak, Laura's face soured, and with a hard swallow, she asked Alex, "Are you willing use your ability if you, we, need it?"

The question Laura asked rocked Alex; he realized Laura was asking him if he could effectively hurt or kill someone if she needed him to. Alex's hangover was gone, but his migraine was back with a fury.

CHAPTER 11

Alex had to go into his bedroom and lie down in the darkness for a while. His head was pounding. He had asked Laura to come in and softly continue. He needed to understand what happened to Paul and who LJ really was.

Laura quietly resumed. She laid her hand on Alex's arm as she began to talk quietly.

*

Paul and Laura lived in a two-bedroom apartment on the outskirts of Atlanta. Paul had graduated with an engineering degree and found a job in nearby Atlanta, nor too far away from his hometown of Hoover, Alabama. Laura had graduated with honors from the same business program as Alex and worked in banking. While the job was boring and rigid, it paid well, had little overtime, and she was able to have much time to herself and her planning with Paul.

Back at their apartment, a week after their face-to-face and phone meeting, Paul had called LJ every single day, against Laura's wishes. To Paul's dismay and Laura's approval, LJ did not answer once, nor was their an option for Paul to leave a message. As the week progressed, Paul became increasingly agitated while Laura felt slight relief and hope that LJ was gone for good. Unfortunately, for her, on the seventh day, Paul finally got his call back.

"LJ!" Paul nearly shouted in excitement. Lately, Laura had been grappling with a perplexing thought: had Paul undergone such a rapid and profound transformation that he was now almost unrecognizable to her, or was it she who was finally awakening to the reality of who he truly was. Either way, it felt much less like a relationship at that point than a business partnership going in the wrong direction.

"Oh, okay, thanks for finally calling."

Laura pointed to Paul and mouthed, "Speaker phone." He ignored her.

"Great. I'll do that ... so 10 a.m., Saturday. And can you repeat the address?" Paul scrambled for a notepad and pen. Laura looked at him disappointedly but Paul did not seem to notice or care. He hung up beaming and turned toward Laura.

"What the hell? Now you're keeping conversations quiet?

"No, no, no. She said she had only a moment, and I had no time. Sorry!"

"Well, what did she want?"

"LJ wants to meet."

"I'm not going anywhere with her!" Laura had already made her mind up. She did not trust LJ, and that was that.

"That's okay. She actually asked that I go alone. So, all good."

"What? You can't go either!" Laura was still shocked that he possessed such blind spots about LJ.

"Of course, I can, and I am. This is what I've ... we've been waiting for. An opportunity to figure all this stuff out!"

LJ wanted to meet him at an obscure place in southern Tennessee the next morning at ten. She gave him directions to head I-24 East, and she'd text him around 8 a.m.; it was a nearly four-hour trip.

"Paul, don't you see this is nuts?"

"Listen, I will text you throughout the day with information; you'll know what's going on as soon as I do. It's going to be great ... I just know it!"

The next morning, he had risen early, and while Laura stayed in bed, she had not a single moment of sleep. She tried to convince Paul after the LJ call to understand the seriousness of what he was walking into, but he wanted none of it. He was going to follow through, no matter what Laura said or did. She wanted to threaten to leave him, but that was petty, even if it was a real threat. So, she stayed in bed and only rose when she heard the car start and roll quietly out onto the street. She waited around the apartment the entire day with her phone on the highest volume setting, waiting for a text or email.

Finally, around 8 p.m., Paul's number sprang up on her cell.

"Laura." Paul sounded slightly out of breath. Or upset. She was not sure yet.

"Paul! What the hell?"

"I can't talk to you very long. Because they said they can't trust you yet."

Laura's worst fears were coming true. "What do you mean, *they* can't trust me yet? What's going on … are you okay?"

"I'm okay. They want to talk to me about you. They told me a few things. And I hope they are wrong. I hope they're fucking wrong …"

Laura felt sick and scared. "Paul, what did they say?"

Paul's voice was shaky. Laura wasn't sure if it was fear, if he had been running, but it was not the Paul she ever heard before. "They told me your father is a glower."

Laura quietly shook her head while her gut sank. She had been hiding her father's ability from Paul because deep down she was not sure she could really trust him. But now he knew and had found out from someone else. On top of all of that, she believed her father's life was now at risk. She wanted to run away. Mustering up courage but not answering him, she said, "Paul, please come home. Just come home now."

"Laura, they're not right, are they? You would never hold that back, would you?"

Laura wanted to do this in person. Explain, or at least try to explain why she did not—no, could not—tell Paul. She would tell him that she could not ultimately really trust him. *Shit*, she told Alex without barely knowing him. But at least with Paul, she could lessen the blow by saying she was scared, which was partly true.

After what seemed like an eternity of silence on the phone, Paul finally spoke.

"It is true, then. Wow. I can't believe you didn't tell me. This is unreal."

"Paul, I'm sorry. Please come home, and we can talk about this."

With a click, the phone went silent. Laura tried to call him back on his cell, but it went immediately to voicemail. Paul never avoided a tough conversation. He was a fighter and liked challenges, but maybe this was too much for him. Perhaps this betrayal was too much for him. Maybe what he felt was right, but there must have been some part of him that understood—it was her dad, after all.

*

Sitting on the deck on a cool morning, Alex looked at Laura in near bewilderment. This was all surreal for Laura, and she could only guess that Alex felt completely lost, as she did. The fact that she was still recovering from too much wine the previous evening did not help.

"That's the last time I heard from Paul. I called and texted him incessantly over the past week or so. He never came home or called or texted … nothing."

"Did you go back to Tennessee to try to find him?" Alex asked, hoping she did not.

"No. I have no idea where he went. He did not let me know where it was, and LJ only told him the exact address only when get got into town."

"Do you think he's okay? Or just really mad at you?"

"I don't know. I think he's in trouble. I mean, I know I should have told him about Dad, but Jesus Christ, he has to understand...it's my *dad*. But I do think Paul's in real trouble."

"And your dad? Is *he* okay?" Alex assumed, or hoped, and asked anyway.

Laura's mom and dad were on vacation the past two weeks. Her dad had won a president's award for being his company's top salesman this year, and they had won a trip to Hawaii for a week and then extended it an additional week.

"He's fine. I've been texting Mom every day for the past two weeks."

Her mom told Laura that she was elated that she had suddenly taken an interest in her parents again. But she also thought it was odd to come back out of the blue like this. Laura had not been part of their daily lives for many, many years. But all in all, her parents were good, for now. "They are flying back to Seattle tomorrow."

Alex showed relief. At least they only had to worry about Paul. *And LJ.*

"Okay, so, your folks are fine but no idea about Paul. What's the plan? What are you thinking?"

"I don't know, Alex. That's why I'm here. I don't really know what to be doing with myself and how to help Paul. I don't think my parents are in danger, but they could be. I'm stuck."

Alex looked like he understood. Finally, after a moment's thought, "Should we try and tell your dad about any of this? Is that crazy?"

Laura had thought about this very thing for a very long time, and while she wanted to talk with her dad for many years, it always seemed futile to even try. However, things had changed, and she might have no choice if her instincts about LJ were correct. She was not yet ready to do so, but she felt that time was coming soon, probably very soon.

Laura and Alex were sipping the coffee, and the sun was starting to warm up the cool morning. They sat deep in thought, trying to make sense of where to start to help Paul. Laura's phone buzzed loudly. She picked it up and saw that it was an unknown texter. She motioned for Alex to come read it with her. She tapped on the message and after involuntarily threw the phone on the floor.

She felt like she was going to collapse. She starred at the phone on the floor. Alex didn't have time to read it before it went flying, so he picked it up from the floor, turned it over, and read the text.

"I'm going after your father. Don't get involved. Stay away and you'll be fine."

CHAPTER 12

Laura and Alex realized their lives would be forever changed from this moment on. Laura nearly tossed the phone again in anger, and dubiously wondered if this was Paul. It was obvious that he was not happy with her, but this text made little sense.

"Laura, would Paul really do this?" Alex asked, apparently on the same wavelength as Laura.

"I don't think so. Was it really him? It was not his phone number. Of course, he could be using another one. Was it LJ's group making it look like Paul? Trying to set him up for something bad? I don't know what to think."

She was rambling and rattled, but Alex nodded, and by his demeanor, Laura felt he understood. They both agreed they needed to change and decide what they needed to do next. Still, their minds raced.

"Don't text or call your parents. Your ... our phones might be bugged. And shit. *They* might know you're here. We need to get rid of our phones." Alex called from down the hall.

As Laura changed, she felt surprisingly calm. They now had a plan, and the threat against her father was horrible, but no longer did she feel indecisive. She needed to help her dad. *Now.*

They regrouped in the kitchen. Alex finished making coffee, and both eyed their phones like they were infected, or worse, about to explode.

"Okay, let's quickly write out all the cell numbers that we'll need. Then, let's destroy these phones and get out of here quickly." As the words exited his mouth, Alex felt somewhat in control.

Both wrote a half dozen contacts that they thought were useful or important. Alex had gotten a hammer from a closet; he took his SIM card out first and smashed it with the hammer on the cutting board. He did the same to Laura's. He then hammered both phones to mere fragments, took all the bits, threw them in a garbage bag, and would later throw them in a dumpster far away from here.

"Okay, great. Now what?" Laura asked.

"We have to get new phones at a store. Lots of them. Cheap ones and we'll just continue to throw them away after each use."

Laura had seen this in many TV shows and movies and always thought that it was not terribly effective and or efficient. If someone had the technology to triangulate their position, then they would have to be very quick in getting out of that location so they would not be caught. But it was a better plan than she had.

"We obviously can't fly. They, whoever the eff they are, will likely know immediately. That's like a fifteen-to-twenty-hour drive," Laura said.

"Okay, so we go get phones, then drive to Seattle."

"What time are your parents arriving from Hawaii?"

"Around 3 p.m."

"We should be able to get there in time if we leave soon."

Laura nodded.

"Shit. Couldn't they detect my car's GPS?" Alex felt like the words out of his mouth were not his, or at least not really something he thought he would be ever saying. Laura and Alex sat at the kitchen table and looked at each other. Laura quietly asked, "Are we overreacting? Is this crazy?"

Alex sipped his coffee before looking Laura in the eyes, said. "I don't know what's going on. This is all insane. But someone just said they're after your father. So, I don't care if we're crazy or not. We have to do something."

Laura got up, took two steps to Alex, bent over and hugged him tightly. "I'm so glad I'm here with you. Now what?"

"We need another car. I'm going to ask one of my pals to borrow his. It's an old car with no modern technology and no GPS. He's nearby. I will give him my car, and I'll take his. I'll make up something like you have some infatuation for old Mustangs. Sound good?"

This on-the-fly planning was new to Laura, but she felt Alex's ingenuity was rather impressive. She smiled, and Alex was caught off guard by her sudden shift.

"Why are you smiling?" Alex asked a bit tersely, regretting it immediately, but Laura paid no attention. She laughed a little and said, "You're pretty good at this."

*

Alex wanted to smile. Wanted to say *ahh, thanks*. But he did not think he was good at this; not even remotely. He began to suspect that the old Hollywood films, with their often misleading portrayals and themes, were influencing him to make choices that left him feeling neither warm nor fulfilled. He did not want to get anyone killed because of his inexperience and ineptitude. Still, he was thankful to see Laura smile. Finding both her boyfriend and dad in trouble was more than enough for him to deal with, and he wondered how she was keeping her shit together. He gave a half-faked smile and said, "Stick with me, kid, and you'll be all right."

Laura laughed harder this time. Alex joined her. It reminded him of their conversations many years earlier about sitting in church. While most everyone at church acted serious, religious, and uptight, both of them always felt giddy and often got a case of the giggles, much to the chagrin of most of the churchgoers. This laugh felt like being at a church. Totally inappropriate, but boy did it feel good. Except, this was not in some holy place or on some holy ground. This was entering into a shitstorm of epic proportions, and both had no idea what was waiting for them.

Alex, muting his laughter, said, "Once we start driving, you'll have to tell me about what you said earlier yesterday. About people 'managing this' gift. I might need to use it, maybe soon."

Alex noticed that Laura was on the brink of tears, her relief palpable. In that moment, for the first time, he truly accepted the reality of the curse, and Laura seemed almost overwhelmed by their shared acknowledgment of its existence.

*

After leaving the house, they threw the remains of their phones in a dumpster. After purchasing a few cheap old-school cell phones with cash from a pawn shop, they proceeded to drive to see Alex's friend to exchange cars. Laura thought that Alex's friend would be eager to learn more about this exchange of cars, but it was rather quick and questionless. She was thankful for boy conversations and interactions; sometimes she yearned for the time to just have stuff work without questions. *So far, so good*, she thought.

Once they got the car, early in the afternoon, they began their northern trek to Seattle. Laura's parents were expected to arrive at the airport Monday afternoon at three, and that meant they had a full day to get there. They had both withdrawn as much cash as possible from ATMs, and Alex had retrieved a stash of cash at his condo. Although they both longed to engage in more trivial pursuits, they diligently prepared as thoroughly as they could.

An hour outside of Los Angeles, Alex asked Laura again about the initial conversation with LJ. "You mentioned earlier that LJ said you can control the glowing? Did she elaborate?"

"Not really. Paul had only talked to me about this once, and he didn't have much to say. He basically told me that LJ says something can be done to mute the ability."

"Hold on." You're saying that a drug can stop it?"

Laura shrugged, "I don't know. That's all he really told me. So, I don't know if a drug mutes it or helps the person control it better. I don't know if it's just therapy or brain surgery. I really don't know anything."

Alex felt Laura's frustration, but he too was frustrated. For the next several hours, he asked Laura about the people and stories they had collected over the years. Alex felt like there just had to be something to be gleaned in them that could help them understand what he and her dad apparently had. Story after story sounded the same and were mostly similar to what Alex had heard from her and Paul's personal narratives.

"So, what do you know about LJ?" Alex was prodding for something. Anything to help understand what was going on.

"We did as much research as we could on her. She's originally from Colorado. Graduated with a PhD in physics."

"Nice, we're dealing with a big dummy?" Alex joked. Laura did not smile.

"And not much else. Very little on social media. Very little on media at all, save for a few awards for schools and business. She's a research specialist for NASA, whatever that really means. No prior records. No husband or kids. Owns a nice but small house in Huntsville. Drives a Subaru."

Alex envisioned LJ to live in a mischievous, dark, and venomous world. Not driving around in a safe and reliable automobile, living in a quaint home. Something felt strange about this.

"Though she did lose her father when she was young."

"What happened?"

"In an article we found on the internet, he died of a tragic heart attack...in a local fair. She apparently watched him die."

Alex thought this might be relevant to LJ's story.

"So, didn't you and Paul think maybe this is part of why LJ does what she does?"

"We think it might be, but we couldn't find anything out. It might be, or it just be a sad tragedy."

Alex's gut was firing; this might be something that changed LJ forever, a question he knew had to be answered at some point. "So, who is this group that she runs or is part of?"

Laura did not know - she knew surprisingly little. Both of them stared quietly at the road ahead and only started again once they refueled the car.

Even after six hours, Alex was still feeling spry enough to continue to drive. The sky was clear, but the sun was starting to set. Neither Alex nor Laura had talked for the past thirty minutes. Laura had closed her eyes and was nodding off. Alex was glad; she was undoubtedly exhausted. With Paul missing, and now her father in some kind of danger, she had every reason to be.

Alex used this silence to process everything. His thoughts kept delving back to something that crossed his mind many times the past day—whether he actually could use his "gift" if the situation called for it. Although he now believed that this stuff was real, he still was not sure if his was, or at least, whether he could ever conjure it up and use it on demand. Could he really hurt someone else? If it meant helping Laura, he had no doubt that he could use it, or at least would try. And he always felt somewhat of a low-level rage way, way beneath the surface. If a situation arose where he needed to end someone's life to save someone else, especially Laura, he'd try with all his might.

Alex was getting himself worked up just thinking about what might be necessary. He started thinking about Paul - he was the one who helped push this mess. Ever since Paul came into Laura's life, Alex's life had become less tolerable and Laura's more miserable. Now, Paul had put her and her family at risk. Alex was burning hot thinking of it all. Miguel and LJ simultaneously flashed in his mind. His mind was racing when he was startled by Laura's loud voice.

"Alex!"

CHAPTER 13

It started when she noticed Alex sighing heavily. She had asked him if he wanted her to drive, but he said he felt good enough to continue. She closed her eyes, thinking of what they had discussed. Her mind drifted to her dad and mom. She was holding her herself together for Alex, but she was about to lose her mind. Her right hand had been shaking for a good hour now, and she kept it out of sight so Alex would not worry.

She really had not slept well for well over a week. Her eyes were heavy, and her mind felt groggy. At that moment, in the car, her body felt heavy, and her thoughts were starting to drift off. It felt wonderful. She absorbed the vibrations of the wheels against the road and listened to the wind hiss from the old car's windows. Her body sank deeper in the seat, and she felt a warm glow wash over her. It was almost magical. She had not felt like this for a long time. Strangely, though, the air was warming, too quickly. A bead of sweat formed and rolled down her forehead. The welcomed calmness quickly became rising agitation and anxiety. She was not sure if she was dreaming, but she was burning up. With a jolt, she opened her eyes, looked at Alex and screamed, "Alex!"

*

Startled, Alex jerked the steering wheel right and almost ran the car off the highway. He pulled to the side, put the old Mustang in park, and turned off the engine. His hands were trembling, and he finally noticed he was holding his breath. He turned sheepishly toward Laura and saw fear sat firmly in her. He was glowing. He knew it. For the first time ever, he felt it in his bones—and it was terrifying. As he looked at Laura, it was easy to see that she had seen this way too often in her life.

"Are you okay Alex?" Laura almost pleaded.

"Yeah, I'm okay."

"What happened? Laura stammered. "I was falling asleep, and then everything went really effing hot. I was almost burning up."

Alex saw that Laura was visibly upset. He started the car again, looked over his shoulder, and pulled back onto the highway. With a deep breath, he collected his thoughts and began to explain.

"Well, I was thinking about how messed up all this was. How your life, and well, mine is so intertwined with this affliction. I started to work myself up about it all. I sometimes do that; I work myself in this internal frenzy and madness."

Laura nodded and listened intently, scared though eager to know how this was working within Alex. He continued, "And I started thinking about how you met Paul, and that was pissing me off." Laura nodded. Alex wondered if Laura really knew how he felt deep down inside. He wasn't sure, but as usual, he was not about to share it right now.

"I was zoned out driving and thinking about all this crap. Then ..."

Laura turned and stared out the passenger window. Alex was embarrassed. He was not really sure who or what LJ was and what she was really capable of, if anything, and whether Paul was a problem or just pissed at Laura for hiding the full truth. This was all too uncertain and yet felt nearly fatalistic. He was not enjoying this road trip; it was a trip of and to uncertainty. Finally, after a few moments, Laura turned to Alex and said, "You know, I never felt that type of heat before."

"Really? Were you ever this close to someone who was glowing?"

"Maybe not this close, but close enough to my dad before. And to you at the bar years ago. But this was different. It was *hot.*

Alex did not know what to say, nor was sure it mattered. Laura continued, "Well, even though you scared the living shit out of me, I'm glad this happened."

Alex glanced to his right with a quizzical look at Laura.

"Hear me out. First of all, you didn't hurt anyone. And maybe I shouldn't have stopped you. But you didn't do or say anything. Second, at least now you kind of know how to bring it on."

Alex smiled weakly at the phrase "bring it on." *Sure. Bring it on and fuck someone up.* He let out a slight laugh. Laura was really funny at times, especially when she did not mean to be.

"You think this is funny, Alex? Huh? Do I make you laugh?" Laura was smiling now too. The stale, tense air finally was escaping the car. Laura continued, "So, we should practice getting you good at this."

"What?"

"I can stop you before you say anything about anyone."

"Get me to glow?"

"Yes, just get you worked up enough so I can see you glow, or apparently now, *feel* you glow."

"Hmm."

"I've never felt that kind of heat before. Maybe it was just my mind telling me to wake the fuck up … who knows? But we'll know soon enough. Let's getting you shining, baby!"

Alex was game, though he was not sure if he really was into this as much as Laura. She had always observed those afflicted from afar. She had told Alex that she never was able to get into the inner workings of those people. But Alex was her guinea pig now, her test subject. He felt a large lump in his throat, and his stomach was in knots. But part of him wanted to try. Who knows—maybe he, or it, could someday help someone in need.

Over the next three hours, around two-thirds of the way through the drive to Seattle, Laura would try to *light up* Alex. He thought this was funny when he first said it to Laura a few hours ago, but after unsuccessfully achieving anything close to glowing, he was frustrated, tired, and hungry. They agreed that they needed a break and stopped at the next station to fill up the car, use the bathroom, and grab some snacks for the road. Alex finally let Laura drive, as he felt exhausted. They agreed to delay the testing for a couple of hours so that Alex could rest.

"You get some rest. I promise, I'll poke you in the gonads if you start to glow."

Alex lightly chuckled and laid his head against the vibrating window, and gently closed his eyes. In the darkness of the night, with the drone of the tires and the faint but sweet smell of Laura's perfume, Alex drifted quickly off to sleep.

*

Laura's mind drifted toward her parents. She and Alex would get Fred and Mary away from the airport and to safety. *But then what?* How was she to tell them of this crazy, screwed-up story? How could she look her dad in his eyes and tell him he's afflicted and he's hurt and inadvertently killed people? Her parents would likely think she was crazy. Even when she told her dad about what he said in the past and what happened to those poor people, he would be annoyed and chalk it up to pure coincidence. She did not blame him for this. They had not been close for the past fifteen years.

She had avoided them both, especially her dad, since she was young. When she left high school, she noticed that they barely communicated with her. They called infrequently, and when they did, she most often spoke to her mom. Her dad was often *busy* and in the rare opportunity he would get on, it was always a short conversation. She assumed that years of her avoiding them had caused a substantial gap in their familial relationship. In the past, she had actually been somewhat thankful for this. It was too hurtful, scary, and sad to be around her dad. Fathers were supposed to protect their daughters and families. Her dad, though, could not be trusted. It was not of his doing, but it happened - might still be happening - and that was something Laura continued to struggle with. She felt terrible sadness in her soul for being so far apart from her parents. But now was an opportunity, she thought, to maybe right the ship.

She was not sure, though, how this was all going to work. She anticipated a lot of confusion and turmoil emanating from her mom and dad when she would eventually try to explain what was happening. There was a real chance her dad would never be able to look at her the same way again and frankly, might disown her. Laura realized that no matter what happened, she had to tell them to save them, even if it meant she'd lose them.

CHAPTER 14

Paul was not yet ready to die.

He had a lot of time to think this past week and concluded he had far from lived a long, full life. He had recently realized he had been consumed with his and others' gifts or afflictions. Only this week had he called his own an affliction; it had led him here, and thus the term *gift* was not appropriate anymore. It was the reason he ended up in this horrible situation.

He was thinking, of course, of Laura; he could not get her out of *his* mind and didn't want to. He always thought of her as beautiful, smart, caring, and strong, but felt it immensely these past few days. He had been consumed by his work and largely ignored her over the past year. But now, tied up and lying on a cold floor in some abandoned warehouse, he realized how he had pushed her away. He wished he had done so many things differently.

He wondered if Laura was safe. He started to pray a couple days ago, even though he never really believed in God. He hoped she was far away, though preferably not with Alex. He felt a big pang of jealousy; Laura never talked much about Alex, but when she did, she *looked* different. Paul knew she held some deep connection with Alex and sensed she had missed him very much over the years. But if she were with Alex, at least let her be safe.

Before he was thrown down in this dungeon, LJ had told him news that shook him almost as much as her disregard for his life. Laura's father was a glower. He was dumbfounded that his girlfriend of many years, his likely wife-to-be, would hide something so monumental from him. Laura had to realize that this put Paul at risk, besides the obvious lack of trust she had in him. He tried to talk to her about it, but before she could really explain, he hung up in utter rage. He wished that he had handled that phone call better. He had a right to be mad but now realized that she was protecting both him and her father.

He was on this floor for what he guessed was several days. He was bound tight by the hands but was able to walk to the small windows and around the mostly empty room. It had a closet that contained a toilet, so he was able to relieve himself. The room smelled like an empty warehouse, musty like stale cardboard. He guessed it may have been a packaging warehouse in the past. There was a very dim light in the room, and he was thankful for that. He tried to count the days, and his best guess was seven nights had passed. He had not received any food or water for what seemed like an eternity, and while he was losing focus and energy quickly, he was surprised that he was still alive. He did not understand that despite his fatigue, he could hang on this long with no food or water. Now, sitting up on the floor, resting against the wall, he thought back to the moment when he chose to go see LJ without Laura.

*

LJ only wanted him and not Laura, and he complied without a lot of consideration, and of course, without Laura's agreement. When he met LJ the first day, she was aloof. She did not say much, and Paul basically felt judged and untrusted. He was eager to find out what LJ and her team were about and how he could be part of it. During the second meeting, the following day, she asked Paul to meet her at an old, decrepit warehouse on the outskirts of Huntsville. After many years of trying to learn more about glowers and sensers, Paul finally felt like this would be his time.

When he got to the abandoned warehouse, he did not see any cars or people near the building. In fact, besides one adjacent building that was nearly identical, the entire area felt eerily quiet. The GPS did not detect the address accurately, so he had to drive around a few times just to figure out where it was. Once inside the unlocked building, he wandered around, looking for LJ. There were three levels and he checked each one. There was nothing in the building but some old furniture. Strangely, most of the doors were locked to what he guessed were offices. He wandered for about twenty minutes, and after a few unanswered texts sent to LJ, he decided he had enough. He walked to the exit and toward his car.

As Paul got to his car and started the engine, his phone rang. It was LJ.

"I am here, LJ. Where are you?"

"I'll be there soon, Paul."

"Okay, I'll wait."

"Yes, good. Before I get there, there's one thing you need to know. And you're not going to like it."

Paul swallowed hard and listened.

"Laura's dad is a glower. I'll be there soon." LJ hung up abruptly.

Paul's face was frozen in distress. He was reeling. He could not imagine the woman he loved kept such a big, dark secret from him. He got out of the car, barely able to breathe, looked at his cell phone, and called Laura. It was not the conversation he wanted, and after a minute, Laura confirmed what LJ had just told him. Paul hung up, went to the door of the warehouse, and kicked it. He let out a loud scream of frustration and decided at that point, he need to go back home and figure everything out with Laura. He now knew why Laura was so apprehensive with LJ - her father was a glower. He knew at some level that why Laura was, but he was pissed. Heading for his car to leave, he heard a voice behind him ask,

"Paul, where are you going?"

Paul turned around, and LJ was just inside the doorframe of the building. He wondered how in the world she got there and assumed she must have come from inside one of the locked offices. He did not like the feeling he had, but he was relieved, nonetheless. "I was just about to leave."

"No, sorry. Come in and let's talk." LJ was a little more upbeat than their phone call minutes before. And Paul, while still upset from Laura's betrayal, felt immediately better.

Paul followed LJ to the second floor of the warehouse, and LJ walked toward a locked office at the end of the long hallway. She unlocked the door and held it open for Paul. He walked though, and she shut the door behind them. There was a small round table with two chairs.

"Sit, let's talk," LJ ordered Paul and pointed for him to sit. Paul sat down obligingly.

"So, you want to be part of something big, right? Something that will help you save the world? Help this world get rid of the glowers? That's what you call them, isn't it?"

Paul thought, *No, I call them shiners, and Laura thinks of them as glowers*, but he did not say anything. He immediately sensed LJ almost accusatory aura. Her eyes look militant and tone of voice felt sterile yet forceful. He was beginning to question the very reason whey he was there.

"So, yes or no, Paul?" LJ asked firmly.

Paul, taken aback, responded, "LJ, why are you so aggressive? You know I want to help, but I don't want to 'get rid of them,' as you say."

As he said that, he noticed shadows outside the door. LJ, staring intently in Paul's eyes, said, "Pay no attention; they're with me. They're here to make sure you have the right intentions."

Paul felt way in over his head, but he carried on. "Okay, what do you mean by intentions?"

LJ sighed impatiently, stood up, and said, "Listen, Paul, this is going to be very simple."

Paul swallowed hard. He knew he was not going to like this. "Okay. Go ahead."

"So, you think you know Laura. You've been with her for a long time. Well, you don't know what you think you know."

Paul's breathing was labored. He was still reeling from the news LJ gave him moments ago, and from the abrupt call he had with Laura, and his subsequent hanging up on her. His mouth felt like it had not tasted liquids in a year.

LJ continued, "She's been lying to you. For years. You and Laura have been tracking glowers for years. You have worked so hard to try and to keep Laura safe and to minimize threats. But you couldn't see what was right under your nose."

Paul's fear was starting to get to him. His right leg was shaking ferociously. He was sweating. But he was also very curious. He waited patiently, and LJ was smiling wryly.

"Laura has known her father was a glower for many, many years."

Paul shook his head in shock and disappointment. It was as if someone sucker punched him square in the nose, and he could not make sense of what was going on him around in a moment. LJ laughed out loud, seemingly loving Paul's distress. He could barely deal with the information but was clear enough to say, "So, what do you want from me?" When he said it, he immediately regretted it. Of course, there was nothing good coming from this question.

"Eager Paul. So eager. Here it is. You have a choice. You need to leave Laura; she obviously cannot be trusted. And if you do, you can join me and our group. We can figure all of this out together."

Paul was hurt deep by the obvious betrayal by Laura but kept some composure. "Why do you care if I leave Laura?"

"I need to trust somebody wholeheartedly to be part of what I have been building. I do not trust Laura, and by proximity, I cannot trust you. In fact, having you here is threatening the exposure of both me and my organization. You're either in or you're not."

"What the hell does that mean?" Paul asked, growing angrier and more confused by the moment.

"Well, Paul, what's your answer?"

"Go screw yourself. I don't give a shit that Laura didn't tell me. And even if I did care, I'm not going to betray her for you!"

LJ turned, opened the door, and two large men in suits walked in with guns pointed at Paul. *Goon one and goon two*, he thought. The smaller one, with a scar on his left cheek that looked a bit too raw, went behind him; he grabbed Paul's wrist, and when Paul struggled, the second rushed at him and hit him square in the face with the butt of a gun. Paul fell to the floor, losing consciousness. On his way down, just before he passed out, Paul thought of Laura. Before fading out completely, all he could think was that he needed to warn her.

CHAPTER 15

A day ago, Fred and Mary had received a text from hell. The evening before their flight back to Seattle, Fred and Mary had planned a splendid meal at a high-end local restaurant. The sun, beaches, and a few too many piña coladas had been a delightful respite from the misty climes of Seattle, but they knew this escape had to end. After all, their trip wasn't just a work venture or an extended vacation, that's what they had led their daughter to believe.

While Mary was showering, Fred heard the buzz of his phone. He glanced at the screen to see a message from an unknown sender: "Laura has been aware of your secret since her childhood. Now, we're also in the know. Await further instructions."

When he read this, Fred dropped the phone and started to shake slightly. Tears were welling up in his eyes. His greatest fear just came to life. His child, his daughter, his only little girl, the one person in the world he was supposed to protect from his awful secret...*secrets*. But, she had known of his affliction. He was completely blind to it for all these years and spent over a decade pushing her away to protect her. Despite his efforts to shield her, she knew anyway - she probably always knew. It was a gut punch. Fred sat down, held his head in his hands, and fought back heavy and deep sobbing.

Before Mary finished showering, Fred pondered the past and wondered when Laura had sensed who he really was. She probably, no, definitely, knew that he had hurt people. Did she know that he *didn't* know? His mind raced with fear and anguish.

Fred's mind quickly drifted back to the fateful day when he found out about what he was and what he had done. Many years ago, he brought Mary out to dinner celebrate and lament Laura's move to Boston for college. He had felt proud of Laura. She was, by all accounts, a wonderful child. While they were not terribly close, and Laura seemed to hold her distance towards him, he always loved her. She was intelligent, worked hard, responsible – a child any parent would be proud of. But he also felt very sad that she was leaving. He wanted to have the relationship with her that was more open and loving, but that time had passed, and he would have to wait.

As they sat in the dimly lit corner of their favorite Italian bistro, twirling comfort pasta on their forks, Mary and Fred pondered the prospect of growing old without Laura nearby. They talked about how they could try to stay connected with her over time.

"Honey, I'm gonna to miss Laura." Fred saw the sadness in Mary's eyes as she softly spoke.

"Yea babe. Me too." Fred replied with a heavy voice with a mix of sadness and regret. He typically did not mince words and wished, at least this time, he offered a more comforting shoulder for his wife.

As the conversation continued, and what so often happened with Fred, conversations inevitably would lead down a darker road. He despised his quick emotional escalations, a trait he inherited from his father – a reminder that the apple never falls far from the tree.

Mary then brought up the neighbors – the ones we never got along with, the ones who always seemed to have a problem with Laura. Mary, usually so reserved, would quietly label them as downright unpleasant. Fred just called them assholes. They were the type to endlessly brag about their own kids, destined for greatness, while implying that others in the neighborhood, Laura included, were somehow falling short. Fred, feeling a familiar stir of resentment, resolved then and there that something needed to change - not just with how they dealt with their overbearing neighbors, but perhaps in reconnecting with Laura, to bridge the growing distance they so deeply regretted.

As Fred's resolve to bridge the gap with Laura solidified, Mary, in a rare display of persistence, dwelled on the issue. Her anger was palpable; she regretted not being more assertive with the neighbors. Meanwhile, Fred felt his own anger mounting, fueled by Mary's uncharacteristic agitation. Seeing her this way ignited a fire within him, an intensity he had experienced way to often.

In a brief moment of silence, Fred and Mary's emotions spiraled into a frenzy. Fred's blood pressure skyrocketed, prompting Mary to snap out of her negative thoughts. She grasped his hand tightly and massaged his forearm, trying to soothe him. But her efforts were in vain. His anger intensified, his face turning a deep shade of red, his body radiating heat. Mary, despite feeling a peculiar sensation that was not fear, for Fred was usually a gentle and quiet man, noticed a flicker of fear in his eyes. On the brink of unleashing a tirade of curses and threats to invisible adversaries, Fred was stopped in his tracks by a hand on his shoulder and a calm, firm voice: "Don't say anything. Please, don't say anything."

A single, unexpected tear trickled down Fred's cheek as his body quivered with emotion. Beside him, Mary was also trembling, mirroring his distress. Turning around, Fred found himself face-to-face with an elderly, diminutive woman. Her kind eyes and warm smile radiated a comforting aura. Speechless, he was momentarily frozen, not by fear but by an overwhelming sense of encountering profound wisdom. Later, Mary confided that she had experienced the same inexplicable feeling.

The elderly lady gently placed her other hand on Fred's shoulder. In the prolonged silence that followed, Fred gathered his thoughts before finally breaking the stillness. "Ma'am, would you mind sitting with us for a while?" he asked, his voice soft yet earnest.

The old lady responded in her sweet, caring voice, "I cannot stay. But I just want you to know a couple things."

Fred turned his chair around a little so he could be face-to-face with this lady. Mary leaned in closer to be sure she could hear everything.

"Sir, you have the ability to hurt people, and until now, you didn't know. I can tell you do not know."

Fred felt a wave of apprehension, not due to the kind presence of the elderly lady, but from an innate sense of the importance of her words. Every fiber of his being urged him to listen, to heed whatever wisdom she might impart.

"You glow very brightly before you say something that will hurt someone. I'm sorry to tell this to you, but you very likely have hurt many people. Likely, some of them have died."

Fred and Mary were listening intently, but the last words made their brains hazy.

"So, when you go home, do a few things. Think hard about the past, what you might have said, and what was done. Come to understand that, and then never do it again."

Fred and Mary nodded reflexively together.

"And one last thing. There are people like me who can see this. Some of those people do not do good things to people like yourself. I can see you are good people, for the most part, at least. Please try to control yourself, sir, for the sake of you, your family and those you might harm." Her eyes were fixed on Fred.

The wise old lady, still holding Fred's shoulder, squeezed it gently, and turning, left the restaurant. A tall lady with blonde hair waited for her at the door. She took her hand, and they both left the restaurant.

*

Mary emerged from the shower, donning her robe, anticipating a pleasant Hawaiian evening with Fred. However, as she entered the room, she found him at the end of the hotel bed, his head cradled in his hands, a clear sign of distress. Sensing trouble, she sat beside him, gently placing her hand over his. With a mix of worry and tenderness in her voice, she asked, "What's going on, honey? What's wrong?"

Fred wordlessly picked up his phone and handed it to Mary, the ominous text message still displayed on the screen. Mary glanced at it, her reaction instantaneous. With a mix of shock and disbelief, she flung the phone onto the floor and began to weep. Fred wrapped his arms around her, offering silent comfort. After a few heart-wrenching moments, Mary, through her tears, turned to him with a determined look. "We need to leave first thing in the morning," she said firmly. "We have to get to Laura immediately. And we need to ensure we're all safe."

CHAPTER 16

Paul was starting to lose his mind. He was sure he would die here and that it would happen quite soon. It seemed like days since he had eaten a morsel of food or drunk any water. He knew he probably should have felt worse physically, but mentally he was losing it. They left him to die, that he was sure of. He was lying on the floor with his hands tied behind his back. He had slept there for a while, and surprisingly, he was not terribly cold. He tried kicking the door handle many times, but it would not budge. The small window was barely larger than his head, and seemed to be much thicker than normal windows. At one point, he screamed so much he lost his voice. Paul began to realize that was a futile endeavor.

In what felt like his final hours, at least physiologically, Paul decided that it was this time to go all in. He did not think he could make it another night, and he realized he had to free his hands, no matter the cost. He knew the time had come, right now.

Paul started to wiggle his wrists. He surmised that if he could just pull, or rather rip one hand free, then he could figure out how to get out of there. The ropes that held his hands were really tight and offered little wiggle room. While his hands felt frail, they felt thinner too. Given that he was right-handed, he pulled with his head, shoulder and left wrist with all his might. He experienced an excruciating, shooting pain in his wrist and shoulder, but he didn't care. This was life or death.

He kept pulling and then started to scream as pain shot through his hand. Paul felt the side of his left hand crunch a little and felt warm blood flow down his pinky. He pushed his left thumb toward his fingers. He continued to pull, feeling the skin burn. He assumed he was ripping through the skin; he had his eyes closed in fear of stopping. But he did not stop. Tears were running down his cheeks, blood was running down his hands, and pain traveled throughout his entire body. But he did not stop.

Finally, his left hand broke free. He brought up his seemingly mangled hand to his face and let out a loud cry. It did not look funny or feel funny, but something in that moment escaped Paul, and he laughed. Though It hurt mightily, and he was certain something was broken, but when he saw the blood and charred skin, he felt luck was finally on his side, finally.

Paul stood up gingerly, wobbly from slight dehydration and aching muscles. He was on to his next problem - how to get out of the room. There window was too small and the door was locked from the outside. Paul walked over to the door, drew in as much air as possible, and with his right leg, kicked as hard as his frail body could at the doorknob. Two more kicks, and the knob fell off and the door jarred open.

He wondered why he did not do this days earlier, as it seemed much easier than he anticipated, but he was nonetheless grateful.

Paul walked out of his captivity room, blood running down his hands and adrenaline pumping through his veins. Even though he felt starving and thirsty, he was already planning his next steps: get out of there, get in contact with Laura, kill JL and her thugs. The clarity was refreshing, and he finally felt clear and right about his mission. He walked carefully to the stairwell, as quietly as possible, even though he'd made a massive ruckus back in the room. No one seemed to be in the building, but he still proceeded cautiously.

When he got to the first floor, he spied the common area and nearly ran to the front door, fully expecting it to be locked from the outside. It was not, and a new relief poured over him. He left the building and followed the road. He waved a car down, and a good Samaritan screeched to a halt, opened the door, and shouted, "You okay, man?"

Paul nearly cried out in relief. The Alabamian native did not ask too many questions and drove Paul to the nearest hospital, just outside of Huntsville, about twenty minutes from the condemned warehouse.

In the hospital, Paul made up some half-assed story that he was lost in the woods on a hunting trip and got his hand caught in a trap. Apparently, the hospital workers had seen similar things in the past and didn't ask many follow-up questions. He reasoned that he might seem like a lunatic with his story and frankly thought the police could put undue notice onto him.

Paul was determined to get mended quickly, get the hell out of there and get home to help Laura.

It was late morning when he realized it was Wednesday. He was surprised that only a few days had passed; he swore he believed he was there for much longer. The hospital staff provided him food, water, and an IV, and he had been able to take a shower. They did not have clothes for him, but the hospital gown felt like a reprieve, and he started to feel a bit like himself.

In the early afternoon, while the nurses were changing shifts, he decided it was his time to move on. He wanted to get home and protect Laura. When he arrived close to his house, he asked the cabbie to drop him off a block away. He had to scope it out, just in case LJ had her goons watching it, as he presumed they would know by now that he had escaped. After careful review, he went to the back entrance of his modest two-bedroom home and opened the doors to his house. That he still had his keys and wallet in his jeans was a surprise. He wondered why LJ and her cronies were so reckless, but again, he was thankful.

He was expecting to see Laura inside waiting, probably fuming about where he had been all this time. He had not seen her in well over a week. She would be beyond mad. But Laura was probably in dire straits worrying about him. He quietly went room to room, but Laura was not there; he briefly panicked, thinking LJ had gotten to her as well. He went to the bedroom and noticed her travel bag was gone and let out a large sigh; he surmised she went to one of two places – to her parents or to Alex.

Paul took a long, hot shower. He was exhausted but there was no time to rest. When he got dressed, sat at the kitchen island, and while engulfing a sandwich, he contemplated his next steps. LJ was keen, cunning, and had ways to know where people were. Calling LJ from his house or cell was out of the question. She had left Paul's wallet and keys in his pocket but had taken his phone. He knew better than to use his credit or debit cards, as they could easily be tracked. He and Laura had left a bundle of cash in a hiding place in their home in case they needed to go incognito. This was as good as time as any.

Paul's brief state of relief quickly transitioned to anxiety about not knowing where Laura was and if she were safe. Frankly, he was sure he was not safe. He attempted to calm himself a little; he was alive, and that had been very uncertain only hours ago. His hand was still throbbing, but it was not just the pain from the raw skin; it was fear flowing through every vein in his body. He also realized his ambition put him in this predicament and it put his life and Laura's in peril. His head throbbed more than his hand.

He figured out a plan, or a semblance of one. He would go find a payphone; there were still some in older malls in the area. He would try to call Laura's parents, Laura, and Alex. Find out what was the situation and then figure out the next steps.

*

At a nearby strip mall, Paul finally found a working payphone. The South was generally very protective of its' history, and for that, he was grateful. He called Laura's mom first, but it went almost directly to voicemail; her dad's phone did the same thing. Both Laura and Alex's phones went straight to voicemail. Paul was starting to feel frantic; he called Laura's mom back and was about to leave a message when Laura's mom picked up the phone.

"Hello?" Mary answered.

"Oh, thank God, Mary! It's Paul."

"Hi ... Paul ..."

Paul could sense Mary's apprehension. He did not want to scare her, but he knew he had to warn her and Fred. "Mary, where are you and Fred?"

"Paul, is everything okay?"

"Yes, no. I'm so sorry. I'm calling you from a payphone because I lost my cell phone; actually, it was stolen, but that's a long story."

Mary did not speak. Paul thought that was unusual, but everything felt unusual right now.

"Are you guys safe?"

Mary stayed quiet. Paul continued. "Please be safe. If you're home, you might want to lock your doors."

"Paul, everything is fine. We're in Hawaii and leaving soon to go back home."

"Oh, thank God"

"Mary, is Fred there?"

"Yes, he is." Mary again sounded apprehensive; Paul could hear her voice and feel it through the phone.

"Please put him on speaker," Paul asked.

"Okay ... done. Fred is listening now."

Paul took a deep breath; held it and released it violently. He sensed Fred and Mary holding their breath. Paul started, "You guys are in danger. Laura is in danger. I don't know where to start, but I needed to tell you that."

Silence. Neither Mary nor Fred said anything. Paul was taken aback. The horrible thought that LJ might have gotten to them already crept into his mind.

"Mary and Fred, have you heard from someone? Has someone threatened you? Please talk to me."

After a long moment, Mary finally said, "Paul, did we just receive a text from you?"

He hung his head and finally was able to respond. "No. Shit. What did it say? Never mind. I want to but I can't tell you everything – it'll take too long. But I was taken to a warehouse by this lady, LJ, and this group kept left me to die. I managed to escape. They took my phone and probably texted you with it."

Fred nearly jumped into the phone and shouted, "Paul, what the fuck is going on?"

Paul swallowed hard. "I don't really know, Fred. Laura and I were ... well, I can't get into the why. But Laura and I were surveilling this person, and she apparently found out.

"Paul, what are you talking about?"

"Fred, please listen. This person, these people, they basically told me that if I weren't on their side, you, Mary, or Laura would be in grave danger. They gave me an ultimatum, and I told them to go screw themselves. I managed to free myself yesterday morning."

Paul was almost pleading for Mary and Fred to believe him. After a moment, Fred spoke. "Well, Paul, that's similar to the text we got."

Paul sighed and asked, "Jesus Christ! What did it say?"

Mary said, "Its says, *I know about Fred. I know all the bad things he's done and who he hurts. And Laura has seen it all. She knows. You're all in real trouble.*"

Mary was quietly sobbing as she spoke.

"Nothing else?"

"No."

"Fred, Laura never told me about you. I only heard about you from LJ last week. Laura was obviously very protective of you."

Paul was ready for the phone to go dead at any moment, sensing Fred and Mary were at their wits' end, and he was unsure if they even really trusted him.

Paul swallowed hard. "Laura is in danger. And you might be in danger too, Fred. You and Mary."

"Okay, Paul, we know! What do we do now?"

Paul could hear Mary sobbing; he realized he was likely the catalyst for all of this turmoil. He buried the thought and continued, "Where are you now?"

"We'll be home in Seattle tomorrow at 11 a.m. We need you to warn Laura. We all need to be together and figure this shit out."

Paul answered, "Okay, I will fly there right away. It's risky, but I don't care."

Paul had thought of them tracking him, but he was not worried about it at this point. "I'll try to find

Laura, but she's not home, and her suitcase is gone. I haven't seen her in over a week. I think she might have gone to California to see Alex. I'm not sure, but I'll try to keep reaching out to her, though they're not answering any of my calls. I'll call you when I get to the airport. Please be safe."

"We'll try and get hold of Laura. See you in the morning, Paul."

Paul felt both a sense of purpose and a gargantuan pit in his stomach. *Where's Laura? Where's Alex? Were they threatened too? Do they know Laura's parents were threatened? Do they think I'm in on it?*

Paul had gotten a taxi to his house, went to his bedroom, lay on the bed, and rested his eyes. He was tired but wound tightly. His brain could not let go of the thought of Laura. He needed to get to her before LJ did. Her life depended on it.

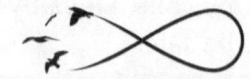

CHAPTER 17

Laura and Alex had finally arrived at Sea-Tac Airport and had several hours to prepare their plan. During the final few hours of their drive, Laura had tried to create the glow within Alex, but he could not access it. It was exhausting. And, it was soul crushing because he knew he was disappointing Laura. They had taken turns driving and tried to get some needed sleep to relieve the extreme weariness. However, the moment they parked their car inside the terminal, his adrenaline was cooking, and Laura looked suddenly rejuvenated as well.

Once inside the airport, they thought of disguises to make themselves less evident to LJ, Miguel, or whoever the hell was a risk to them. Given that they were dealing with professional adversaries, or at least someone who knew more about them, they felt ill prepared for their undertaking. While they decided a disguise was ultimately useless, they nonetheless resolved to purchase a couple of baseball caps and hoodies, to at least entertain the thought that they might be less obvious.

Quickly but quietly traversing the airport, they located a small restaurant outside Terminal 2, where they sat in the back corner, facing toward the crowd but away from the foot traffic of the day's travelers. After grabbing some much-needed coffee and nourishment, Laura looked at Alex and asked, "So, what's the plan?"

Alex sighed deeply reflecting his deep level of concern. "Well, I checked their flight. They'll be arriving at eleven a.m. It's nine fifteen. I was thinking you call them as soon as they land. Tell them to come directly to this terminal—forget about their bags. Tell them to not look around, not be nerv—"

"Hey, I know you're excited, but slow down a bit." Laura said abruptly. Alex's mind was speeding up, and Laura looked worried. "I'm sorry, but just take a deep breath."

Alex heeded Laura's words and inhaled deeply, then slowly let it out. He was anxious and his mind was spinning, but it helped.

Laura did not wait for Alex to continue. "Okay, so I'll call them on one of our throwaway phones. Tell them to meet us here? They have to come straight here and not to the bag check area, right?

"Yes," Alex answered.

"Okay, good. So, I'll have to make sure I don't scare them too much, and hopefully they'll listen to me. I'll tell them the truth, or at least part of the truth, for now. That we are all in danger, and they can't argue, question, or anything. Just listen and do what we ask."

Alex could see the tension rise in Laura. He knew that her parents might very well not listen or at least not hear what she had to say. As time was of the essence, he nor Laura could not let them sabotage their own safety.

"Okay. Once you get them to agree to come, we'll get them in the car and take off. We should be okay, if we can get a head start. We'll be safe in the airport, but we'll need them to be able to slip by whoever these damn people are."

Every word Alex said felt foreign, and his tongue was heavy. He was in over his head, but now there was no other choice but to soldier on.

After Laura processed Alex's words, she added, "We'll give them these hoodies; at least it may make them less visible. Probably not, but we'll try. We'll meet them in the bathroom; you with Dad and me with Mom. Then we'll leave together. We'll have to tell them to ditch their phones, tablets, computers— whatever they have."

Alex nodded. This was not going to be easy or fun.

Both let out large, nervous sighs.

"Alex, what if they just tried to scare me … us? What if they, whoever they are, are not even here?"

Alex nodded. He had played this scenario over several times on their way here.

"Well, we can't take that chance. And my gut says they are here. Better to be safe than sorry."

Laura nodded. One hour and counting until Laura's parents would be landing. They sat in silence, sipping their coffees while time crawled by at an agonizing pace.

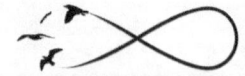

CHAPTER 18

"Laura, it's time to call them. The plane should have landed by now." Alex was determined. Laura nodded, and she called her mom as Alex called her father. Several rings. Nothing.

Laura and Alex were waiting impatiently near the coffee shop, and with each passing moment realized how open they were to the world. They both scanned the area continuously but saw nothing out of the ordinary. Alex was sipping his black coffee. Not that he needed to be any more aware than he felt at that moment; he presumed he would never feel this alive ever again. A nagging doubt somewhere deep in the recesses of his mind knew that he was likely wrong.

Laura was getting frustrated and nearly shouted at her phone. "Jesus, Mom, answer your phone!"

Alex responded, "They're probably seeing 'unknown caller,' so they're probably ignoring them. Let's text them."

Alex and Laura texted them simultaneously. Just a quick one to say it was them and then they both called them again.

Laura's mom picked up. When Laura heard her voice, her body exhaled like she had been holding her breath for days. She felt for a brief moment almost normal, though she knew that wouldn't last for long. Her mom started to babble. Laura couldn't get a word in. She tried to tell her to stop talking, but she kept going.

*

Fred and Mary were holding hands as the plane touched down in Seattle. Not because they were so in love; they were, but that was not the reason. Not because they hated flying; they were not complete fans of it, but that was not it. They were genuinely scared that something bad would happen to their daughter. They also both feared that she would hate them; all these years living with knowledge of Fred's curse must have been hell for her, and she must have held a deep resentment in her heart. Fred held Mary's hand tighter, and she put her free hand to his cheek and spoke softly. "We'll be okay, honey."

When the plane landed, they turned their phones on, and almost immediately both of them rang. No caller ID. Maybe it was Paul again, but of course he could not be calling both at the same time. Was it the bad guys? Was it Laura? They had to make a choice quickly. They would not answer.

They collected their overhead belongings, waiting for the line to start moving so they could exit the plane. Nervous energy and a sense of dread filled them. Their phones both dinged with an incoming text message. As they slowly walked down the aisle, Mary reluctantly read hers first.

"Mom, it's Laura and Alex. Please answer your phone NOW!!"

Fred immediately opened his text, and it said the same thing. Almost immediately, both phones rang again; Mary picked up, and Fred ignored his.

"Laura?" Mary asked cautiously.

"Oh my God, Mom. Yes, it's me."

Mary's knees almost buckled when she heard her daughter's voice. Leaning in close to Mary and the phone, Fred had to fight back tears; *there's a time and place, and it's not on a plane in front of all these people*, he thought to himself.

"Mom, we have only a few minutes. You have to hear me loud and clear, okay?" Laura pleaded.

"Yes, Laura, but you need to let me say something really quickly. I know you know about your father. We've known for it for years and just found out that you knew all along. We know we're all in trouble. You. Us. Paul. And likely Alex. We know you have a gift, that you can really see people, like your dad. And we know Paul can too. We know, and we are so sorry."

Mary waited for Laura to respond but heard only silence. Fred was looking at Mary with hope and fear. Hope that Laura still loved him or at least forgave him for what he had done and put her through. Fear that she would not.

*

Laura was back to barely breathing. The words pouring out of her mother were near earth shattering. Her mom knew so much. Laura's gut instinct was to hang up and throw the phone away, but she finally took a deep breath. Alex was listening carefully and while unable to hear everything, he got the gist of it.

He looked at Laura, then looked up at the ceiling and exhaled. Then he gave two thumbs up. Laura shook the cobwebs out of her brain and was finally able to respond.

"Jesus Christ, Mom, you just saved me a lot of time and anxiety. We have a lot to catch up with when you're ... *what the fuck* ...?"

*

Mary recoiled. The phone went dead. And then nothing.

"Laura? Laura?" Mary was terrified. What the hell happened? Fred was barely able to contain himself, and Mary instinctively held his hand. The door up front in the plane was open, but the line barely moved. Fred was frantically waiting for the line to speed up, and Mary knew what would come if he got too excited. She held it closer, leaned in, and said, "Just breathe, please."

Then Fred's phone buzzed. It was a text from Alex.

"Fred. Alex here. I'm with Laura, and she's fine. Don't go to baggage claim."

Then a text buzzed on Mary's phone from Laura.

"Mom. Read carefully. Go to the arrivals section, and in the first bathroom you see near The Coffee Spot and meet me in the bathroom. Have Dad do the same. Go straight there! Now!"

*

Laura was about to tell her mom the game plan, when out of nowhere, a man had walked directly in front of her. He was wearing a hat and dark glasses. She almost screamed at the phone and hung up on her mother. She could see Alex out of the corner of her eye, moving quickly in front of her. Alex was *glowing*.

The man put his hands up as if to say, *I'm not here to hurt anyone.* Alex was still glowing and waited for the next move. The man put his hands up to his head and slowly pulled the hoodie down to his shoulder. Alex's eyes flickered and Laura gasped. It was Paul. He did not seem fazed to see Alex glowing, but Laura knew she'd have to deal with that in the future.

After an awkward moment of silence, Paul finally said, "Guys, I can't believe you're here!"

Laura finally moved out from behind Alex, glared at Paul, and responded, "How can we trust you?"

"It's a long story, Laura. I will tell you everything, but you have to trust me. They're after you and your parents. And you too probably, Alex. Now I can see why."

Laura felt like a traitor at that point for never telling Paul about Alex. But that was something to deal with later.

"They tried to kill me, and it almost worked. I escaped and was able to get hold of your parents after not reaching either of you. I came here to here to help your parents. And then I was going to try and find you, Laura."

Paul was noticeably shaken and near tears. Alex was still very wary and still glowing slightly. Paul looked at him, smiled knowingly, and nodded as if to say *I understand*. If not for the situation, Laura might have felt relieved that Paul and Alex finally understood one another.

"Guys, they gave me an ultimatum that I turn against Laura - basically disown her. It was stupid and made little sense, so I told them to go fuck themselves. They gave a similar warning to your parents Laura! We need to get Mary and Fred to safety now!"

Alex and Laura looked at each other. Her mom did say Paul was in trouble too, which did not mean a lot at the time, but they now realized they had little choice but to trust Paul. They would get the full story from him later. For now, they had to focus on Mary and Fred. Alex had already been typing a text to her dad. All three of them had put their slight disguises back on. To Laura, the scene was almost comical. Though if felt like a horror show.

CHAPTER 19

Alex, Laura, and Paul were waiting anxiously by the coffee shop for Fred and Mary. Alex's responsibility until then was to continuously scan the area for LJ and likely her goons.

While waiting, Paul stood near Laura. He tried to hold her hand, but she reflexively pulled back. Paul felt lost and lonely but understood Laura's reaction. The days on the floor were way too fresh in his bones and helped provide enhanced clarity to his life. He was Laura's lover, and other than Alex, her most loyal and trustworthy person alive, but nonetheless, he believed that might have already lost her.

"I'm so sorry about all of this, Laura. And I'm sorry I left without you," Paul said quietly.

*

Laura sighed deeply; she did not want to be part of this conversation right now. Too much was on the line. Alex was in front of her, pacing and scanning. She wanted to go hold his hand tightly and ask Paul to leave. She was too confused and tired to truly contemplate what life would be like in just a few hours, let alone in the future.

"Paul, we'll talk about this another time, okay?"

Paul hung his head slightly and nodded almost imperceptibly. Laura felt a pang of guilt. Only weeks ago, he had made her breakfast in bed for their anniversary. She remembered how she felt warm and wanted; had trusted someone more than ever and had belief about a future. Now, she would not, could not, hold his hand. Frankly, she was unsure if she could even trust that he was on her side anymore. But despite her feelings, guilt still flowed through her body and mind.

Paul jumped. He turned toward Alex and Laura and said quietly but with intense fear, "Damn! It's LJ!"

Laura and Alex looked slightly past Paul and saw them too—LJ was intently walking with two large, serious looking men. Collectively, and without speaking, they decided they needed to get out of sight and walked the opposite direction. The found a section that was empty and mostly out of range of normal walking traffic. They all sat down together, and Alex said quietly, "It feels dumb to run away from them. They can't really do anything to us in an airport."

"Right, but I still don't think we need a greeting party." Paul was red - Laura was not sure it was fear or anger. Paul looked different today, and she felt for him.

The three adversaries walked slowly past them. LJ was looking straight ahead. The goons were scanning the place and seemed to look past them. Fred and Mary would be coming the opposite way of where LJ was headed. Paul, Laura, and Alex slowly got up and moved back toward the coffee shop and bathroom. Alex cautiously scanned the path of LJ and her group. They were still walking the opposite way. It was at least five minutes and still no sign of Fred and Mary. Laura looked at Alex and said, "They're not here yet … Jesus."

Paul was about to speak when Alex's phone rang. It was Mary. He picked up.

"Mary?"

"Alex, I'm in the bathroom. Tell Laura to come get me. Fred's in the other bathroom."

"Okay, be there in a sec."

Laura was trying her best not to tackle the phone from Alex. He quickly relayed the messaged and added, "Okay, let's go. Now!"

*

Laura hurried to the women's bathroom, barely a three minutes walk from their coffee shop hangout. She had to fight to not run, and her heart was pounding. When she got there, a line of women formed well outside the bathroom. She looked at the men's bathroom and saw Alex go in unimpeded while Paul waited outside for both. She normally would wait, but she felt like a fish in a barrel. Through narrowing eyes and evil murmurs of the crowd, she pressed on through to the bathroom, quietly saying, "I'm here for someone."

*

Alex had gone in, and while there were a few people waiting for the urinals, he walked past several stalls to check which one contained Fred. He went back to the short line and grabbed his phone to text him. Before he could, Fred had already beaten him to it. "Last stall next to the 'wet' sign on the floor." Alex immediately went over, and the door was slightly ajar. Alex felt apprehensive. It was strange to walk into a bathroom stall with another human being in it. But these were strange times. Fred looked a lot larger and tougher then Alex remembered. He'd only seen him and Mary on a couple of occasions when they visited Laura back in Boston many years ago, and Laura had kept those meetings very short. Alex knew she did this to protect them from one another. Fred waved Alex in.

"I'm so glad you're here and you look okay, Fred." Alex was genuinely relieved.

Both were whispering.

"Okay, now what?" Fred was visibly nervous.

Alex gave a sweater and hat to Fred. It really didn't match the khaki pants he was wearing, but style mattered less on this day. Fred pulled the sweater over his head and put the hat on. Alex nodded. The left the stall and headed toward the exit.

*

Mary had texted Laura that she was in the fifth stall from the window. Laura knocked softly and asked, "Mom?"

Mary opened the stall slightly, and Laura peeked in. Mary started to cry softly and held her arms out for Laura, who hugged her mom tightly and said, "I'm so happy to see you."

"Oh, my sweet girl. I'm just happy to be here."

Laura looked at her mom and passed her a fleece with a baseball hat. Her mom quickly put it on without a word while Laura spoke. "Come on. Let's go get Dad, Alex, and Paul."

They left the stall and headed toward the exit. They looked left and right, but Paul, Alex, and Fred weren't there. They saw no one.

"Oh, shit," Mary and Laura simultaneously murmured to themselves.

*

Paul watched Alex and Laura walk into the bathrooms. He felt anxiety about what was to come but also relief that everybody was no worse for the wear and now all together. They had a fighting chance. He was finally feeling like himself. He scanned the areas close to him but saw nothing. They would not be longer than a couple of minutes, so he felt safe, for now.

Then a voice whispered behind him.

"Paul, don't turn around too fast. And listen to me carefully. If you don't, you know what I can do to you or others."

Paul felt his knees buckle, but he managed to stay straight. He recognized that voice. It had a hint of Latino and a whole lot of southern.

"Miguel?"

Behind him, Miguel could barely contain himself. He chuckled loudly then talked quietly again. "Paul, start walking now. Or I turn around, walk out of here, and make your life miserable."

Paul instinctively walked away from the two bathrooms, away from his friends and lover (ex-lover, he really presumed) because he knew what Miguel could do. They walked quickly, and Paul dared not look back. He wanted Miguel away from all of them.

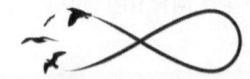

CHAPTER 20

Minutes later, just moments before Laura was planning to barge into the men's bathroom for the first time in her life, Alex and Fred walked out. Laura slowly stepped toward her dad and hugged him tightly; she thought it was risky, but she did not care. Her dad wrapped his hands around her like he might never let go. After the embrace, they convened outside the women's sign, and Alex asked, "Where is Paul?"

Laura and Mary had worried looks on their faces.

"We don't know. We were hoping you would know," Laura answered.

"You know, I'm not sure if we can really trust that guy," Fred said.

All of them agreed internally, but no one replied. Alex finally continued. "Well, let's get the hell out of here. They obviously know we're here, so we have to do this carefully. Let's get to the car. Maybe Paul will be there. And if not, we'll figure it out after."

The four of them looked like a family of rabid sports fans and a bit overdressed for the weather. While the weather was warm, a constant sprinkling of rain provided some semblance of rationale for sweatshirts and hoodies and hats, so they weren't totally out of character for Seattle. While they all knew that it would not be difficult for LJ to recognize them, they still tried to be as inconspicuous as possible. Alex had asked them to all look down while walking and fake talk and smile. This felt odd to everyone, but they nonetheless tried.

They got to the elevators, and Laura pushed the button. No one dared to look back, except for Mary. Alex remembered Laura telling him she was always overly curious and cautious.

"Oh my God!" Mary whispered and whipped around to face her family with force. Fred, Alex, and Laura turned their heads back and saw what Mary saw. LJ and her posse were walking straight toward them.

*

Paul had led Miguel to the parking lot. Twice he tried to spark conversation with Miguel, and twice he was reminded to shut his mouth. On level three, they walked to Miguel's car, and Paul was ordered to get into an expensive Mercedes. Paul wondered what life path Miguel took. He and Laura lost track of Miguel for years; he was hard to find, and with no criminal record, they eventually lost interest in him. Now, Paul knew that the loss of focus on Miguel was a big mistake.

Miguel point Paul toward the driver's seat and ordered him to drive.

"Nice car, huh?" Miguel was beaming. It brought back memories of school to Paul; Miguel always seemed to be flashing that asshole smirk of a smile when they were young, and apparently, he never stopped.

They drove out of the parking lot and onto the highway, and finally Miguel started to talk. "So, what are you and that wretched bitch, LJ, up to? And why are you guys stalking Laura and her family?"

Paul flinched and looked at Miguel quizzically. Miguel noticed it and let out a slight sigh.

"Okay, man. Spill the beans. What's going on?"

Paul was confused. Miguel knew way too much about what was going on yet seemed to also think poorly of LJ. Slightly relieved, Paul responded, "Have you looked at me? LJ did this. Well, her assholes did this to me. And they almost killed me. I barely survived the ordeal!"

Miguel started to laugh, shaking his head almost hysterically. He asked Paul to pull off the highway and pull over. When they came to a stop, Miguel looked at Paul. For the first time, Paul saw what he thought was concern and a twinge of normalcy.

"Okay, Paul, before I fully trust you, tell me the story. The story of you and Laura and why the fuck you were following me for years."

Paul was taken aback again. He was not a person who trusted others easily. He had seen bad stuff happen to too many people. He did not trust Miguel one iota, but when it came to LJ, what did he have to lose? He also needed to get back to Laura, and keeping Miguel engaged felt like the right thing to do. After a moment, he started. Miguel stared away from Paul, out the passenger side.

"You remember the day Laura met you? I mean, first saw you."

Miguel nodded.

"Well, that was her first time trying to find out if she really had the 'gift,' or curse, as she sometimes calls it." Miguel did not say anything or move. He just continued to look at the window. "I was basically doing the same thing, though in reality, I knew of you beforehand. I wanted to see if you'd glow again."

Miguel sighed deeply. Paul was not expecting this type of solemn behavior, but he felt a sense of relief coming from Miguel.

"And when you started to glow, she literally ran onto the field. I think she wanted to help."

Paul saw Miguel swallow hard. He could not read Miguel that well, but at least he seemed somewhat intrigued by the conversation.

Miguel asked, "She wanted to help me or someone else?"

"She wanted to save you ... from hurting someone and having to live with that. She always wants to help people."

Miguel's body relaxed, and he seemed to become less tense. Paul could see that Miguel's eyes were somewhat glossy. It was not something Paul thought he'd ever see.

"That's how I met her. I sought her out after that and told her I had the same gift as her, and I was following you for similar reasons. After that, we tried to find people like you. Not to hurt them or bring them to the authorities. Damn, no one would believe us, even if we tried. We just wanted to help people not make bad decisions. It's a bit naïve, yes, but we really wanted to try and let them know what they were doing. We wanted to do something good."

Paul, of course, was leaving out the fact that they believed Miguel was a bastard and that he actually likes to hurt people.

Miguel finally turned toward Paul. "So, you think I'm a killer?"

Paul recoiled a bit and believed Miguel could see through him. He took a deep breath and answered. "Listen, man, I don't know much about you. I saw you light up a few times during games, and then I read about a couple of players that got hurt, and one died. My shitty research as a child showed you played against them, and the timelines show that it easily could have been you. I never was sure if you even knew about your ability to glow. Most people don't know they have it!"

Miguel looked away again. Paul could not tell what Miguel was thinking. He continued, "But after that night, even though we followed you around for a few years, we never saw you glow again. And we never really pursued you much since."

Miguel rubbed his eyes, though Paul did not see tears. Paul *almost* felt sorry for Miguel. Miguel finally spoke. "I remember her running onto the field. I remember being angry at that asshole on the other team. Or maybe it was the ref. I don't know. Jesus, I can't even remember why I was so mad. I was crazy angry. And then I see everyone look past me, and I turn. This hot chick was tackled on the ground and looking at me. I could tell she was very scared of me. But they were eyes of compassion too. I was only a kid, but I could feel it."

Paul knew that look. Compassion. That was one of the reasons why he loved Laura so much.

"And then I realized she could see me. I mean, she could see what I could do. And it was strange, man. It finally made me happy that I wasn't so goddamn alone in the world."

Paul exhaled a little. He knew that feeling, as did Laura. Miguel looked at him quizzically.

"Laura and I both understand that feeling man. We, like you, didn't ask for this. To try and help people who didn't know they were hurting people is hard. Shit, everyone's hurting everyone all the time—but seeing it happen. Seeing people glow when they're about to possibly kill someone, that sticks with you. That makes your mind and body get real screwed up. It never leaves you."

Miguel nodded, though Paul was unsure how Miguel was processing the information. Paul continued, somewhat reluctantly, "And that laugh you made when you knew she knew. That has haunted her a bit." Paul looked at Miguel almost like he was waiting to be punched or ridiculed.

Miguel laughed out loud and then said, "Oh, man, I really need to apologize to her. I was just so happy that I wasn't crazy and someone else knew what was happening to me. After that night, I have not done anything. I've kept everything in check. It was the night that changed my life."

CHAPTER 21

At the elevator, Fred was shimmering white. Laura stared at him with a mixture of fear and kindness in her eyes while Mary held his hand. Fred look embarrassed for being so angry.

Mary was feverishly hitting the P3 and "close" buttons in the elevator. Laura was now alternating between her dad, LJ, and her best friend, Alex. There was so much she felt at this moment of terror and so much she had not said or done with either her dad or Alex. Her current feeling of disappointment almost overshadowed her fear.

The door would not shut, and LJ and her two bodyguards were nearing fast. Laura noticed LJ's stoic look, and it puzzled her. She expected something else from LJ, something akin to angst or evil. But LJ looked more like a professor contemplating her next lecture.

"The fucking door won't shut!" Mary shouted. Alex and Fred reflexively went to the elevator opening and pushed Laura behind them. LJ was now at the elevator, and Alex stood in front of the four. LJ's foot held in the elevator door from closing, and her two body-guards unexpectedly turned away from the group.

"Get the hell away from us!" Fred said, still glowing brightly.

LJ leaned forward just a bit and softly said, "Fred, relax. I'm not here to hurt anyone. And, well, you can't really hurt me or my friends here either."

Fred did not relax, and nor did anyone else in the elevator, though the tension was easing slightly. No one spoke, and LJ continued.

"You think I'm the bad guy. You probably think I almost killed Paul. Right?" She paused, creating more tension and curiosity.

"But I'm not. I'm trying to help you all. People like us. People like Paul and Miguel. Well, I tried with Miguel, but he's a lost cause."

Laura, Alex, and her parents were listening intently, trying to understand what was happening. They were fearful for their lives yet were confronted by a story that said otherwise. They were not at ease. Far from it. But they did welcome news that made them feel slightly less apprehensive, and scared.

*

Paul convinced Miguel to go back to the airport. He told them of the parents flying in and that Alex, Laura's old college friend, was there with her. He did not mention LJ. He thought that might create too much suspicion.

"I'm going to call Laura and tell her we're on our way back."

"Be careful. Don't mention me yet. It might be too much for Laura."

Paul nodded. *Good advice*, he thought, but Laura would be worried about him. He dialed her number. One ring. Two rings. Paul was already beside himself in fear of what might be happening to Laura and her family. After a some futile attempts, he called Mary.

*

Mary's phone rang, and her family, Alex, and LJ turned toward her in anticipation. LJ quickly asked, "Is it someone important? Is it Paul? He's with Miguel."

Laura was stunned. How in the world did she know so much? She seemed to know everything that was going on. And did she know about Alex? No one but her knew about Alex. On cue, LJ continued, "We have quite a few other teammates here, guys. They saw Miguel and Paul walk out of here. We believe Miguel threatened him. Pick up the phone and tell Paul you are all safe and you'll call him back."

Laura took the phone from her mother, but did now yet answer.

"But are we? Are we really safe?"

LJ showed signs of frustration but continued, "Let's all go back to the airport and find a cafe. I will tell you everything I can. We're all safe at the airport. But you probably should call or text Paul back. He might be in trouble, or he and Miguel might do something stupid."

Alex finally intervened. "We're not calling anyone until we know what the hell you're talking about. We don't trust anyone, especially you."

LJ took a visibly deep breath, and after a moment, she replied, "Okay, we're heading to the cafe we passed a couple minutes from here in this terminal. Come meet us there. Don't leave if you want to hear what we have to say. But I've had enough of convincing you we're on your side. It's your choice now."

With that, LJ turned, and the three of them walked casually away.

*

Paul texted Laura and her mother while he drove back to the airport. Miguel did not seem to mind the illegal and risky maneuver of texting while driving, and Paul thought it was wise enough, given the situation. His gut was telling him that LJ had captured them all. He wished he had the power to hurt LJ from here. He did not, though Miguel did.

"Miguel, I think LJ has Alex, Laura, and her family. I need you to glow and glow now."

Miguel started to laugh.

"Why are you laughing, man?" Paul was almost panicky now.

Miguel turned to him and spoke softly. "Paul, I get that you're worked up. But I guess you don't know, right?"

"Know? Know what, man? Don't leave me hanging!"

"Yes, yes. You know, I can't hurt those who shine or glow, right?"

Paul shook his head and turned toward Miguel.

"Wait. What are you talking about?"

"I told you earlier after I saw Laura on that football field, I never hurt anyone. Well, that was true but it wasn't from lack of trying. LJ is a total bitch and she made my life a hell for a while. She threatened my life. Beat me and left me for dead, like you. She wanted me to join her crazy batshit group."

Paul realized he and Laura were not the only ones harassing Miguel. LJ had gotten to him and nearly killed him as well. He thought that maybe, just maybe, Miguel could be more a victim than a perpetrator.

"So, of course, I tried many times to hurt her. But it never worked. And honestly, Paul, I've tried with you too after I knew you were stalking me. But it never worked. And it won't work on LJ, even if I tried."

"So, you're telling me it won't work on those who can see glowers?"

"Right."

"And how about those who glow?"

"That I don't know, but I'm assuming not. Otherwise, LJ's crew would have put a hex on me a long time ago."

Paul looked worried.

"Well, maybe it just hasn't happened yet. Maybe it takes longer to get through, or something like that."

Miguel countered, "Sorry, man, that was four years ago, and I tried too many times to count. Glowers can't hex glowers or those who see."

Paul stepped down hard on the gas pedal and said, mostly to himself, "We need to get back to the airport."

*

The elevator door finally shut. The four of them stood quietly for a few minutes. Alex started. "There's no goddamn way in hell we go to them. It's a trap or a trick or something. Something bad will happen."

Fred and Mary nodded in full agreement. Laura stood and did not join them in affirmation. Her face was showing signs of stress, lack of sleep and, much to Alex's worry, doubt. Alex reached out to her shoulder and asked, "What's wrong?"

The elevator door opened, and everyone turned toward the door with anticipatory anxiety. A collective sigh was released when there was no sign of LJ or Miguel. They stepped out onto the P3 floor, where Alex's friend's car was parked. The all stopped about four steps out into the parking lot when Laura answered Alex. "I'm not sure what is happening. I'm not sure if we should leave here without talking with LJ."

Alex was visibly frustrated, though he tried to contain it. Her dad was not so withholding.

"Jesus Christ, honey! She threatened us. She threatened you and Alex. She damn near killed Paul. What else do you need to know?"

Laura nodded to acknowledge that what her dad was saying was not wrong. She just could not shake this feeling.

"Guys, no matter what we do, they'll be haunting us and probably hunting us forever. We'll never get to the bottom of this. We'll be living our life looking over our shoulder. I'm not doing that. I'm sorry. We can live in constant fear, or we can deal with it now."

Fred was about to go off again when Mary held and squeezed his arm. He stepped back and looked away. Mary asked Laura, "Honey, what is it? Why do you think we can trust them? Why shouldn't we run?"

Laura turned her back toward the three of them. Alex sensed what Laura was about to say.

"Mom, Dad, I feel like I've been running my entire life. Running away from you both because of what Dad could do. Running from places where I see bad stuff happening. I am tired of having bits and pieces of information, and I feel like I can't sit still. I need something to be resolved. And I'm tired. Really tired." Laura's phone vibrated with a text from Paul.

"Guys," she said, "it's Paul. And he's with ... Miguel!"

Alex and Laura were visibly stunned, and Fred finally asked as they all stood in the parking garage, "Who the hell is Miguel?"

After a deep sigh from Laura, she answered, "Dad, Mom, it's a very long story. I'll fill you in later. Right now, I have to go see LJ."

Alex could barely contain himself. "Laura, let's call Paul first and get his story. We can't dive into this headfirst!"

Laura looked at Alex with impatience. "We can't hide. There's no hiding. We're safe in the airport. Nothing will happen there. We can call the police if something does. We'll shout and scream if need be. But we need answers, and I think LJ will provide at least some of them."

Alex was shaking his head. He was nearly distraught and could feel anger swelling inside. Breathing deeply, he finally said, "Okay, well, all right. I guess there is no stopping you. But let's call Paul on the way."

Laura nodded. Mary let out a slight "aughh," and Fred held her hand tightly. Laura looked at them both and said, "Mom, Dad, why don't you leave. Throw away your phones now, so they can't track you. Take the keys to this car ... they can't track that either. And pick up a few disposable phones. Make sure you write all of our phone numbers down first, though. Get a hotel room, and pay cash only. Text us only in a few hours, and we'll update you.

"Laura!" There was uncertainty in her dad's eyes and fear in his face.

"Dad, we'll be fine. Nothing is going to happen to us here. Plus, if anything does, we'll let you know, and you can help ... call the police or something. But get somewhere safe, so we don't have all of us in harm's way."

Fred and Mary nodded. Mary was visibly holding in a burst of tears and Fred looked like he might start glowing soon. It was strangely familiar to Laura, but this time she was not mad or frustrated or sad at either of them. This time she knew that they were victims as well, part of something they really could not understand or mostly control.

Laura hugged her mom and dad together while Alex waited. Laura then grabbed his hand and said, "Let's go."

CHAPTER 22

P aul and Miguel arrived back at the airport. Paul was visibly nervous and frustrated, as no one was responding to his texts or calls. The parking lots were nearly full, but by the time he shut the engine off, Paul's phone finally rang. He picked up without looking at the caller ID.

"Laura!" Paul nearly shouted.

Silence. Nothing. Paul shouted her name again. And then a woman's voice, but not Laura's.

"Hello, Paul. Glad to hear you're doing well."

Paul nearly dropped the phone. Miguel looked at Paul and saw the blood drain from his face.

"Who is it, man?" Miguel asked.

Paul gathered himself, ignored Miguel, and spoke almost too softly, considering who it was. "What is wrong with you?"

Silence from LJ made Paul steam with rage. He supposed that that is how all this shit started; the rage he was feeling now is what glowers must feel before they screw someone's life over. At that moment, he wished more than anything to be a glower; though, of course, he knew from Miguel that was effectively useless for people with the gift, or curse, of glowing or sensing.

Finally, LJ continued. "Paul, I know you must hate me. But listen to me carefully. You're in real danger. You might think I'm full of shit, but what we did with you, it was a test. I had to be sure I could trust you. I had to be sure you were strong enough and resilient enough to deal with the shitstorm that's ahead of you; of all of us."

Paul was not having any of it. He looked at Miguel, who was squirming uneasily and shifting in the passenger's seat. He mouthed, "Who is it?" Paul thought Miguel looked both terrified and angered. Paul shook his head and kept his focus on LJ. He turned the car toward the side of the road, put it in park, and pointed a single finger without looking at Miguel, to signify he would only be a moment. He was keen to not alarm Miguel any more than he had to. He finally replied to LJ. "You got thirty seconds."

"Paul, I can't tell you on the phone. I'm in the airport, and Laura is on her way to speak to me. Come to the coffee shop that was near Fred and Mary's terminal. But Paul, watch out for Miguel. He's dangerous. Very dangerous. He and people just like him are the reason we exist. The reason why you thought you were going to die in that warehouse. So please be ..."

Paul felt a jolt to the back of his head. All of a sudden, he felt very sleepy. He struggled to keep his eyelids open, and as he turned toward Miguel, with his consciousness barely holding on, he realized what had happened. Miguel was looking at him with rage, and the blood splattered on his face, *his blood*, was glowing brightly. Before Paul could feel any more terror, he passed out.

*

Walking to the coffee shop to go speak with LJ, Alex and Laura tried to call Paul back, but there was no answer. Alex's gut was turning relentlessly, and while he felt invested in protecting Laura, he secretly wished he was somewhere else. Nothing seemed to be going well, and people, including Paul and Laura, were constantly making poor choices. By proxy, he felt like a true enabler.

"Laura, are we doing the right thing? LJ is probably a murdering psycho. She almost killed Paul! And what the hell is Paul doing? He hasn't stop calling and texting and now is ignoring us. I don't like this."

Alex could see the anguish Laura was feeling and knew that despite her insistence, she was doubtful about the decisions she was making.

"Please trust me, Alex. I know this is all crazy, but I've been around crazy my entire life. But I agree; I don't have a good feeling with Paul right now. I hope he's okay."

Alex nodded. They were just about at the coffee shop when both could see LJ and her men sitting at a rectangular table, with two empty chairs. They were all sipping coffee simultaneously. Alex didn't fancy himself a whiner, but he tried just before engaging with LJ one last time, "Laura ..."

"We're doing this."

The two walked quickly to the table, and even though LJ was not looking their way, she got up, turned around, and guided her arm for them to take a seat at the table.

"Coffee?"

Laura was taken aback. "We're not here for pleasantries. You've been making my parents' and ex-boyfriend's lives a living hell. What the hell is going on here?"

"Sit down and let's talk. Guys, please leave us. Stay close and keep a lookout. Miguel may be around." Her two bodyguards stood up and slowly walked away.

*

Laura felt to her core that Paul was in trouble. She started there.

"What is going on with Paul? Is he really with Miguel now?"

LJ nodded her head with what seemed like genuine concern. Laura continued, avoiding Alex's look of disappointment and bewilderment.

"I know he's in trouble. He came here to help us, and then vanished. What happened?

"I literally just called him, and as I was talking with him, the phone just hung up mid-sentence. That means Miguel knows I was trying to tell him the entire story," LJ told Laura and Alex. She looked concerned, which was not something Laura or Alex had expected. Laura felt dread rise in her body, and when she looked at Alex, he said, "LJ, what is going on here?"

"Alex Connor. You're the one person I know everything about but nothing about. Why are you in this situation? I know you and Laura are friends, but why are *you* here?"

Alex rocked back in his seat just a bit, and Laura looked away. Laura tried to conceal the truth by avoiding Alex, but she felt LJ could see through them both. For his part, Alex remained stoic and answered, "I care. Laura is my best friend. I can't not be here."

LJ nodded. "Well, I'm assuming you either are a senser or a glower. It has to be one or the other, otherwise you probably wouldn't be in this shit. Either way, I'm glad you're there for Laura and her family."

Neither Alex nor Laura reacted to LJ's rationale. They both intuitively knew that it was best to leave those comments alone and let silence speak.

"LJ, can you tell us what is going on and why the hell you're terrorizing everyone?" Alex asked.

LJ glanced at Alex and turned back toward Laura. "This is a long story, but I will try and do it quickly. There is the matter of helping Paul. But I suppose we will be hearing from him soon enough."

*

LJ started from the beginning. Laura had recalled some bits of information from her initial meeting with LJ, and while the story seemed consistent, there was a vital deviation.

"I told you when we first met, I was approached by a group. Well, I was, but it was not a friendly group. It was a rogue group that wanted me as their weapon. They literally nabbed me from the street; kidnapped

167

me and held me against my will. They sat me tied to a chair for days and tried to find out what I knew about glowers and sensers. They hit me a few times, but nothing bad, thankfully."

LJ continued. "The group was, effectively, a mob presence in Tennessee. Their leader had known about glowers and sensers, and likely someone on their team saw a glower and connected me to this person."

"Wait, why would they *want* you? Were you doing what you're doing now? You, know, stalking and threatening people." Alex questioned.

LJ ignored Alex's last part of the question and answered. "No. I was trying to avoid seeing any glowers and living my life. I was just trying to get past it all and try and be normal. But they had different plans. For those three days, they interrogated me. They would... well...well, let's just say they would *sometimes* let me use the bathroom."

LJ's eyes were misty. Laura and Alex showed little empathy, and Laura asked, "Where is this story going?"

"Well, I thought on the end of the third day, I would die. The mob boss comes in with a gun in his hand pointing it at me, laughing. But instead of shooting me, he unties my hands, grabs a cloth and cleans my face and says, 'Okay, you can go.' I didn't believe him, so I didn't move. I wouldn't get up. I didn't say a thing. I just sat in the chair. I thought if I got up, and turned to walk away, I'd be shot in the back. As I sat there quietly, he continued to laugh...like a hyena."

Alex and Laura continued to look at LJ, wondering if she understood the hypocrisy, given what she had done to Paul.

"I asked him, carefully, why he was laughing. He said to me, 'Listen, I can hurt people by just saying it. And I've been trying to kill my nemesis for months... once I found out he also had the touch of crazy. But nothing has happened to him. He's still walking around scot-free. You know how many people I've hurt? Killed? Way too many. But I can't hurt him; at least I can't kill him the *clean* way.'

"I was pretty damn confused, and after three horrendous days tied to that chair, I didn't know what to think. I asked him quietly, *why me*? He answered by saying one of his members saw how I recoiled when he was 'in the zone' while they were in a public location. I never realized that I saw them...him...before but they certainly recalled me. And they knew then I could see what he was doing."

"But what the hell did they want you for? You could never hurt them," Laura asked.

"Right. But they wanted to find out if they could hurt me. So, he basically had me there for three goddamn days to hurt me with his words. He was trying to hex me. I was his testing subject for three day. And it didn't work, obviously."

"And he just let you go, just like that?" Laura was incredulous.

LJ nodded. "Yep. He told me he needed to find out his boundaries. His limitations. So, in essence, I was his guinea pig."

"Why didn't you go to the police?" Alex asked, still not believing all that LJ was spewing.

"Why haven't *you* gone to the police?"

LJ and Alex swallowed hard and looked at each other. They *wanted* to but never believed it would help them.

"First of all, guys, the police might lock me up in the looney bin if I told them my truth. And the mob guy basically told me that if I went to the police, he'd know immediately, and I wouldn't be touched, but my family would be." LJ looked afraid for the first time.

Alex continued to look suspiciously at LJ and asked, "So, are you saying that glowers cannot hurt glowers *or* sensers?"

LJ nodded.

Alex held his breath and wondered if Laura could sense his overwhelming feeling of relief. He always wondered if, at a bad place in his life where he might feel envy or sadness, or anger toward Laura, he would hurt her with his words. Unlike most others, his words could *really* hurt. Part of that feeling and fear created a real emotional gap within Alex that persisted all these years but was begging to be released. If LJ was telling the truth, it was something that would enable him to let go of such fear of closeness he felt with everyone, especially Laura. Alex let out an audible breath when Laura touched his hand; he was not sure she could read his mind, but he was thankful for her being there.

"Okay, LJ, that's all great and shit, but why bother us? Why not tell us this in the first place? Why in the hell would you torture Paul?" Laura demanded.

"I'm sorry again for all of it, but it is necessary. I tried the normal, safe, and *good* route for years, but it backfired several times. You see, those that have the gift of glowing, as you call it, and gift of sensing, often have God complexes. People like Paul are on the verge of, well, teetering on the superiority side. We both know that he wants to be a vigilante of sorts. But ultimately, he does seem to trying to do the right thing."

Laura got up from her seat, and Alex had to hold her back. "Yeah, because you almost killed him!"

"Laura, I understand you're pissed. But you know full well what I'm talking about. Paul got real pleasure in knowing he had this gift. Some people want to make a world of difference and make it all about them and create virtual shitstorms."

"Like you?" Alex blurted out.

LJ looked at Alex and nodded. "Yes, somewhat like me. Paul and I are not much different, really. But I've learned to try and do the right thing, despite the shit I'm in. So, I had to test Paul. You, Laura, I did not. You've always had great intentions; that was always easy to see."

Laura was not buying any of this. "But you almost killed Paul. What are you not getting?"

"No, Laura. We have cameras set up in that room. We were monitoring him all the time. He was shaken, of course, but he was not in trouble. We were about to let him go before he managed to figure out how to escape."

Laura, nor Alex, was buying it. LJ continued before their retort. "Here, let me show you."

Laura and Alex looked at each other, reluctant and shaking their heads. LJ continued. "Please, just look. You'll understand a bit better."

LJ grabbed a tablet from her purse, opened up some app that neither Laura nor Alex recognized. It showed an empty room in a warehouse. LJ forwarded the video slightly where LJ and her goons showed up and where placing what liked like cameras throughout the room.

"Right there, we're putting state-of-the-art technology in the room to get ready for Paul. See the date ... it's two days before Paul arrived."

Alex and Laura were confused, and were no closer to feeling better about any of this.

"We had sensors and cameras throughout the room to measure heartbeat and detect brainwave activity. The infrared lasers are so tiny, Paul would never see them. You can see the activity here on the screen. We always wanted to make sure Paul remained safe." LJ pointed toward the corner of the tablet, showing several graphs and a heartbeat tally.

Though Laura reluctance meter was still running high, she was at least calming down enough to stop thinking about grabbing a plastic fork and shoving it in LJ's eye. But before the video continued, Laura demanded,

"Stop for a second." LJ pressed on the tablet.

"Why do this to Paul? Why not simply sit with us longer than you did? Why not just talk more to us?"

LJ looked away and sighed heavily. "I've been doing this a long time. I used to try that; be reasonable and talk normally with people. But I have had very little success, especially with certain *types* of people."

"Like Paul?"

"Well, yea, similar to Paul."

"So, instead of being human, you terrorize people and make them hate you?"

"It's not that simple."

"Well, it seems pretty damn simple to us." Alex yelled over both LJ and Laura. LJ tried to answer.

"The next step with Paul was to talk to him about the experience and then to you. But we hadn't gotten there yet."

"Well, that seems pretty fucking dumb. You're creating enemies by your tactics, not partners." Laura was shaking her head in disbelief.

LJ pressed play on her tablet and continued. "Here's the day he broke out of the facility. His vitals are fine. He's doing okay."

"Show us!" demanded Alex. He and Laura knew this was not going to end well; neither believed it was really just a test.

LJ smiled weakly. She went back a day on the app and pulled the time to two a.m. Paul was asleep when a man and women walked in with what looked like a medical apparatus and put a needle into Paul's arm. It looked like a drip.

"See, the brain and heart rate are increasing a bit to metabolize the liquids. And here, we're doing a blood pressure check to make sure everything is okay."

"How do we know that you're not just drugging or poisoning him?"

"Guys, come on. I know you have a reason, lots of reasons to be skeptical. But open your eyes."

She again forwarded to the hour he escaped, and then to her team cleaning the room up about thirty minutes later. Alex and Laura looked at each other. Their reluctant facial expressions showed LJ that finally they started to at least consider that this was legitimate.

"Okay. So, if this is a test, and a fucking strange and convoluted and frankly inhumane one at that, so what now?" Alex could not hide his frustration. He was not Paul's biggest fan, but he was worried for him.

"Well, as I mentioned, we were going to sit with Paul and Laura; go through this civilly. But we now know Miguel has something up his sleeve. He's a loose cannon, and we think he might be after you and Paul, and by extension, your family."

Laura intervened. "Mom and Dad are fine. And you don't need to worry about Dad. He's fully aware of what he's done, and he's controlled it for years."

LJ nodded in approval and said, "I know. I met him once before ... my mom and I. But that's for another time."

Laura looked appalled but not completely surprised. She looked at Alex and said, "I don't know what to ..."

Before she could continue, her phone rang loudly. Both Alex and Laura turned immediately to look at LJ. She nodded and mouthed quietly, "Pick it up."

"Hello?" Laura asked, putting the phone on speaker.

"Hey, longtime friend. In the mood for a little game? Not football this time, though!"

Laura's eyes opened wide and dread ran down her face. "Miguel, what are you doing?"

"Laura, my old friend, or is it nemesis? Either way, if you are not here in two hours, your friend Paul will meet his maker. But if you come alone, he'll be fine, and you guys can go your merry ways. I just need to see you. I'll send directions." And then Miguel hung up.

Laura felt overwhelmed. She wished she could glow Miguel to fucking smithereens.

CHAPTER 23

Alex and LJ begged Laura not to even consider this. It was an obvious trap. Miguel was a nut job and he was baiting her in. She and Paul would be in extreme danger, and everyone knew it. Laura looked spent; she looked down at the phone, almost like it might bite her. Alex wondered how she was really coping; today was an epic shit show.

"I'm going, guys, so either help me with a plan or say your goodbyes."

Alex grabbed Laura by the hand, "Can I have a moment with you alone?"

LJ got up from her chair and headed for the coffee counter. Alex felt heat expanding in his bones. His mind and body were beginning to feel the effects of the overburden of stress from the past few days. He was scared for Laura. If there came a time when this madness would settle down, he would pursue his true feelings for Laura. He was not sure what they actually were, but he knew that deep down inside, there was no one in the world more important than her. It did not matter if she would not reciprocate; he wanted to be more a part of her going forward in whatever way she saw fit.

"Why do this? This is, I'm sorry ... just ... crazy. I can't let you go without telling you this. I'm just ... I'm just ..."

Laura took Alex's hand to her cheek and held it. She leaned in, kissed him gently on the cheek, looked him in the eyes, and said, "I have always thought about you. I have missed you for so, so many years. I don't want to let you go. You mean the world to me."

Alex's eyes were welling up. She did not divulge her love for him, but this was the most vulnerable she had ever been. He was fighting the urge to completely break down and sob like a child.

"And if I don't go and Miguel does hurt, you know, really hurt Paul, I'll never be able to forgive myself. I won't be able to live with myself. Remember, I spent many years with Paul, and he's a good man. He has tried to live life right, and really, he treated me fairly, and with love. He'd do it for me without a second thought. I know it's a huge risk to go, but I have no choice."

Alex wiped a tear that reluctantly escaped. Though he was not a typically sentimental guy, today was an exception. "I get it, but I still don't want you to go. Let's call the police."

"You know what Miguel will do to him."

Alex nodded and leaned forward and kissed Laura on the forehead. "Let's talk to LJ at least."

LJ had come back with three new coffees. Alex took one, and Laura glanced at him. "You think you should be drinking that?" she almost shouted.

LJ grabbed Alex's coffee and took a gulp. She did the same to Laura. She looked at them both slightly annoyed and then asked, "So, now you know I'm not poisoning you, what's the plan? I'm assuming you couldn't convince Laura to halt her dumb plan ... no offense."

Laura ignored LJ's insult. She looked at them both and said, "Let's figure something out. We don't have much time."

*

Paul was in complete darkness. Once again, a sense of dread washed over him, a feeling he had come to know too well recently. He could not see the hand he placed out in front of his face, and he tried to shout, but nothing came out of his mouth. He was confused, but he felt someone nearby, slight footsteps walking his way; despite his general fear, he knew this person was not someone he needed to fear. He could smell a sweet, floral fragrance that he'd smelled many times before. He still was unable to talk or shout but he *knew* that aroma; it was Laura's. His heart swelled, and he smiled to the darkness. She kept quietly walking toward him, and finally he could see her. She was eye to eye with Paul, tears running down her face. She looked beautiful and so unlike anyone he'd ever met. But her tears started to turn red, and his heart stopped when he realized it was blood. At that moment, he could feel it trickling down her face; thick, warm blood that filled him with inescapable terror.

He tried to reach out to her and yell her name, but he was frozen.

Miguel shook Paul awake. Paul could feel blood trickling from his forehead. The dream had him shivering, and the reality of the situation did not make it better.

"Laura's not here yet. Soon, but not yet. Oh, at least you better hope she is!"

Paul immediately recalled the phone call and then saw the gun still in Miguel's hand; it was dripping blood. His hands and feet were tied to the back of a chair. *Not again*, he thought. He tried to shake the cobwebs out of his brain and finally asked, "Why did you do this? And what are you trying to do? I thought you were one of us, one of the good guys."

Miguel grinned that evil smirk that haunted Laura for years. Now Paul realized that Laura's instincts about Miguel were not wrong, not one goddamn iota.

"Paul, Paul, Paul. I'm not a bad guy. I just hate most people. Man, don't you know people?"

Paul was wary of what would come next.

"You, Laura, Laura's dad. You're just pawns in my games. I'm after a lot more than your dumb asses. But LJ, she's the real pro. I haven't been able to get near her to do any damage. But for some dumb reason, she thinks all you guys are special. And she thinks I'm a powder keg. Fuck that bitch. I'm going to show her what a real powder keg is!"

Paul felt like he already knew the answer to the question he was thinking, but he asked it anyway. "What did she do to you?"

Miguel's expression turned sour. "Well, I guess you could say she was testing me. She almost killed me. I barely made it out alive. But not before I killed one of her goons. Man, that was fun. And I used my own hands. That was a first for me."

Paul felt sick to his stomach. He felt like this situation was much worse than what LJ had done to him. At least LJ left him alone to die. And now, sitting her in pain and terror, he was quite sure that Miguel had other plans that were much worse.

"You said she was testing you? What do you mean?"

Miguel looked at Paul with curiosity. "I guess it doesn't matter, because it's likely you or I won't be alive after today anyhow. And it's sure as hell not going to be me if I can help it." Miguel laughed way too loudly. "LJ told me after I escaped that she wanted to be sure I would be on the right side of righteousness. But after I killed one of her guards, she said that was impossible. Like, what the fuck is that about? I thought they were going to kill me!"

Miguel was shaking his head violently. Paul was wondering where he was going with this, but maybe his near-death experience was a test too. Even though he Miguel was a lunatic, he could understand Miguel's motives for getting back at LJ.

"I agree with you. This was self-defense. You had to do what you had to do."

Miguel snickered. Paul's innards squeezed tighter. Miguel continued, "Well, I didn't *have* to. I saw that he was in a room upstairs of some old warehouse. I went searching once I escaped that dreaded room. I was looking for revenge. And boy, did I get it!"

Miguel beamed with pride and enjoyment; Paul shook almost uncontrollably and was unable to tear his eyes away from Miguel's psychotic smile.

*

Alex and Laura still had doubts about LJ. Frankly, their level of trust in her was minute. But there was a small problem of Paul being in absolute peril, and that made Laura steadfast in her decision, despite the obvious pitfalls that lay ahead.

LJ then pulled out her tablet once again.

"Before we go, I want to show you something. So you can hopefully trust me a little more … and also know who you're dealing with in Miguel."

Laura was losing her patience.

"Guys, I have to go. The moron texted me his location, and it's forty-five minutes out. I have only twenty minutes to spare, assuming the roads are clear." Thankfully, it was a late Saturday afternoon and not typical workday rush hour. Laura was happy that at least one thing likely would go right.

"This will only take a minute." LJ found her file and pressed play. It was Miguel in the warehouse room, tied up. LJ pressed fast forward, and Laura and Alex saw a similar scene to Paul's. A few moments and more fast forwarding later, they both saw Miguel, as Paul did, escape captivity in what looked like the same room. But unlike Paul, Miguel did not leave the building and run away. The anger in Miguel's face was apparent and very different from the fear in Paul's when had had managed to extract himself. The cameras followed Miguel who, like a stealthy panther, lurked upstairs and slowly walked into an empty room. It was at this point he realized LJ was monitoring him in the room. He suddenly turned around very quickly and hid behind the door.

"What the hell is going on?" Alex whispered as if Miguel might hear him. Laura leaned forward, in a manner that suggests she too was unsure, but absolutely fearing the worst.

A man in a suit walked in, looking downward adjusting his belt and completely unaware of the intruder. Before he reached the TV monitors and chair, Miguel leaped out and hit the man square in the jaw. The man dropped straight to the ground, apparently knocked out, with the back of his head whipping violently against the floor. Miguel then jumped on his chest and with both fists, pounded the man's face.

Laura pleaded, "Please turn this off."

LJ did and added, "His name was Jim. We could not recognize him after this. His wife and children had to have a closed coffin at the funeral. They couldn't make him look like, well ... you know, like Jim."

Alex went into panic mode. He nearly shouted at Laura. "Can we rethink this? He's obviously insane. Please?"

Laura but got up slowly and insisted, "I'm going. I need a car. Now."

LJ nodded and answered, "Okay, we have one for you. Alex, let's you and I drive together. My guys will follow me. We'll talk more when we're on our way."

CHAPTER 24

Laura was driving a large, black SUV alone. She had programmed the address into the GPS screen and had forty minutes to go with fifteen minutes to spare. She had no idea why she was so persistent to go see LJ at the airport, but she trusted her gut. She was thankful she did, as things seemed clearer. Going to try to somehow rescue Paul, on the other hand, was a completely different story. She was not sure if it was the right thing to do, and her intuition currently was not agreeing with her decision. However, deep down, she absolutely knew why she had to do it. She had told Alex that it was because she felt loyal to Paul, and while that was not untrue, in reality, she was doing it for both her family and Alex. She wanted to save Paul and hopefully save her family; if Miguel was to go free, then they would be all in peril.

"Laura, can you hear us?" Alex asked through a bluetooth receiver coming from the large speakers in the car. Laura was surprised by the sound of Alex's voice, but it brought her back to the present moment.

"Yes, I can, Alex. I'm so glad you're here with me." Laura could hear sympathy and fear in Alex's voice.

"I wish you wouldn't do this, Laura. I can't bear to think of anything happening to you."

Laura's heart hurt when he said this. She knew that Alex was only looking out for her, and he was probably right that she should not go to see that madman. It was almost as if she had a death wish. But she also felt angry at Alex; she wanted to focus and be clear minded, and Alex was making it hard. She wanted more support and less doubt. Thankfully LJ had a plan. Her two assistants were driving in a nondescript SUV a few minutes ahead of both Laura and LJ and Alex. They would scope the area out quietly and would be primed to pounce in the room with Miguel, Paul, and soon Laura, *when* the timing was right. Laura knew something bad was going down, and she hoped it would be only Miguel who would be affected.

"Guys, tell me again why it's not good to call the police?" Alex asked LJ and Laura.

A moment passed, and LJ answered, "My two assistants are ex-military. In fact, they're Navy SEALs; they're the best and you're in good hands. The police, well, they could easily be hurt or be killed by Miguel from afar. It's too risky."

Alex shook his head, exasperated. Before he could argue, Laura intervened. "I saw what my dad did. The devastation he caused with the simple words he used. Do we want to put anyone else in harm's way?"

Alex's immediate thought was "hell yes," but he refrained. He was getting nowhere, and his mental fatigue was setting in. He stayed quiet, for now.

*

Laura was driving and thinking about what she would do. She was scared, and that was okay; it meant she was alert. And Jesus, she thought, she needed to be alert; she was going deep into the pit of hell. She was still unsure about this, but she knew she had to do it. Her phone rang loudly again. She left it on speaker with Alex and LJ, so they had full communication with whoever was calling.

"Guys, my phone is ringing. I'm going to pick it up."

"Be careful. If it's Miguel, just say you're twenty minutes out now and you'll be there soon. Nothing else for now."

Laura heard LJ, took in a deep breath and answered swiped the phone.

"Hello?" Laura tentatively asked. Her heart was racing.

"Laura, how are you, sweetie?" Her worried father asked. Laura took it off speaker and nearly started to cry. It had been so long ago that her dad gave her even the slight affection she so desperately wanted. Before today, she had withdrawn from him because of the bad things he unwittingly did. But now, after all she had learned, she finally realized the toll it likely took on him. He had gone to great lengths to protect her from his curse, and she finally felt she had her dad back. She wanted to hold him and tell him that he meant the world to her.

"Laura?" her dad pressed.

"Sorry, Dad. I hear you. I'm just so glad it's you."

"Hi, Laura, I love you, darling," her mother said from the speakerphone. Laura always thought her mom was such a good, kind, loving person. She always wanted to keep the peace; Mary's rock-solid foundation of love and loyalty was what Laura and her father adored. This was needed at this time in Laura's life.

"I do too, guys. I'm sorry I can't talk long. I'm in a bit of a predicament."

Her dad worriedly asked, "What now, hon?"

Laura took a deep breath. She wanted to lie to avoid the conversation and also protect them. But it was probably this type of secrecy that kept them so isolated from one another for so long. "Guys, I'm sorry to say this, but a real asshole of a bad guy has Paul, and we're all going to try and save them."

"LJ has him?" Mary and Fred said in unison.

"Sorry, but it's way too long of a story, and I'll tell you when I get back. Call me tonight. I love you, and ..." Laura wanted to tell them that if she did not see them again, she was proud to be their daughter.

Her dad, showing a side that Laura could not really remember, intuited, "Laura, we'll talk to you tonight. You're going to be fine. You're going to get through this day, and we're going to get back to being a family. I know that. I feel that. And we love you."

*

Alex was fidgety. He noticed how calm LJ was, and it made him simultaneously nervous and hopeful. He knew Laura was speaking to her parents, and though normally he was generally very okay without talking, at that moment, he was lost. He felt things were going to get worse.

"Are you okay?" LJ asked. Alex felt like she read his mind. But this time, she sounded really concerned.

"No. I'm really worried for Laura. And Paul."

LJ nodded in agreement. "Yes. This has gone astray. I'm sorry that this is happening, Alex. We will do everything to make sure nothing happens to her."

Alex was not at all convinced, but at least it was something, he thought.

*

"Guys, it was my dad. He and Mom are good. We have ten minutes before we reach Paul. Any final thoughts?" Laura said.

LJ responded, "You have the knife, right? It's still hidden inside your jacket?"

LJ had given Laura a very small but rather sharp-looking, black-handled, serrated stealth-type knife that felt like it was a specialized army weapon designed for quick and silent operations. LJ had said that when Miguel got close, she might have to use it on him. Laura was not a fan of this option, of course. When patting the jacket down, the knife would be difficult to notice. It might be her and Paul's last shot at getting out of there alive if LJ's men were unable to rescue them in time.

"Yes." She took her right hand and dug inside to feel its icy handle. *What the hell was she getting herself in for.*

Alex said, "You're going to get through this."

Laura swallowed hard, and LJ spoke. "Let's check your earpiece. Check, one, two, three." LJ had set up a very small earpiece for Laura, as well as a small camera on a pendant hanging from a new necklace.

"How is it that you had this technology lying around?" It was an odd question that Laura had thought of, but it made LJ briefly chuckle.

"Yeah, I tend to be overprepared. We keep relevant tools nearby for a just-in-case moment."

"Well, this is definitely a just-in-case moment." Laura felt a small sense of normalcy creep back into her senses.

"Check, one, two, three."

"Yep, it works great."

"Remember, I'll be in your ear. I won't say much to confuse you, but I'm right here, and I'll help you through this. And the camera signal is great. You're in good shape."

Laura laughed nervously. She did not feel like she was in any shape to do any of this, but she knew she must go through with it; she could not handle Paul's death, knowing she had a chance to save him.

"Remember, Laura, try to find an area with a window, and go to that opening. My guy will be positioned if Miguel has really bad intentions."

Laura took a deep breath.

"And what if there are no windows?" Alex asked. He didn't have an earpiece, but the conversations were going through a Bluetooth receiver and car stereo system, so he could hear everyone, and Laura could hear him.

LJ responded, "As soon as you go in, scan the room. If we have a window, go to it. If not, don't worry. My other guy will infiltrate the room at the right time"

Laura took a deep breath. She now was only minutes from her destination.

CHAPTER 25

Miguel was pacing the floor. Paul's bleeding had finally stopped, and the left side of his face was caked with hardened blood. His hands were sore, but he apparently was getting used to that.

"Miguel, why do you want Laura here?"

Miguel stopped pacing and glared at Paul. "Dude, don't you ever shut up?"

Paul looked at Miguel, curious about how he might respond, but also worried that he was pushing him too hard.

"One word, pal. LJ. She has made me want to ruin her world. And I know she's got a big crush on Laura. And I guess I do too." Miguel burst out laughing. Paul was sick to his stomach.

Paul waited. He felt Miguel was losing his shit, though he reasoned that had always been the case.

Miguel continued. "Man, I just want to talk to Laura. Get under LJ's skin and then get away from all of this."

Paul knew Miguel was not only crazy, he was also very inconsistent. When he heard Miguel threatening his life if Laura did not come here, *alone* of course, he had a strange feeling. And as Miguel was threatening LJ, and earlier with Laura, he was glowing brightly. That really scared Paul.

"I get that LJ is a bitch. Damn, in some ways, I want her dead. She almost killed me."

"Paul, Paul, Paul. You're thick sometimes, man. I just told you that I want to fuck with LJ. She won't come for you. She cares more about her nice, hot morning latte then she'll ever care about you. But Laura, she sees something in Laura. Maybe Laura reminds her of a younger version of herself."

Paul continued to listen intently, while trying to ensure that Miguel would be calm when Laura got there.

"And shit, man, Laura loves you! And she will come for you ... she's coming for you! And that means LJ is close behind. You'll see. But don't worry, man. I'll let you both go, and I'll never see you again after today, but without Laura, there's no LJ."

"Why not just get to LJ another way? Something that doesn't require Laura. Laura really just wants to blend in. She doesn't want any part of this stuff anymore. She hasn't for a long time."

Miguel had put Paul directly in front of the small office window, overlooking a patch of grass. A hundred yards away was another similar building. It reminded Paul of an old private detective's office you would see in the movies. It was dark and gloomy, and if he were not in such dire straits, he would probably think it was mysterious and interesting. They were located on the third floor of a four-story building that still had some small-business occupants, but because it was a Saturday, it was empty but for them.

Miguel was pacing, away from the lone window while Paul's back covered most of it. He presumed Miguel placed him there strategically. Anyone trying to take Miguel out would risk shooting Paul. This was a nightmare Paul never dreamt he would be part of, but knowing Laura was about to enter the fray, he was more scared than he ever thought he could be.

"Don't worry, Paul, this will all be over soon, and you'll get another chance with Laura."

Paul managed to keep a stoic face, but inside, he was trembling.

*

Alex's hands were sweating profusely. He felt nearly hopeless knowing Laura was going into hell, basically alone. He should be there with her, he thought.

"Alex, are you okay? You look really stressed," LJ calmly said.

"Well, it doesn't matter. I'm not the one going in there with that madman." Alex was fuming. He was trying to calm himself so LJ would not see him glow, but he was barely hanging on to the fear and rage bubbling inside of him. Only Laura had ever seen him glow, and of course, even if he wanted to, he really couldn't command it if he tried, nor would it work on Miguel. He composed himself and spoke softly. "LJ, is she going to be okay?"

LJ took a deep breath and nodded. "We're going to do everything in our power to make it so." Pressing her earpiece, she said, "Laura, my guys are there already. One is in an adjacent building about a hundred yards away. The other is on the ground behind the building. You'll see him as you enter the building. He won't be far away. And remember, get Miguel to the window. That's our best chance to make sure if anything goes off course, we can minimize the situation."

Laura didn't speak. Alex quietly said, "Laura?"

"Hey, you. I'm a bit scared."

So many emotions swirled in his head. Lying to himself and to Laura, he said, "You're going to be fine."

LJ added right after Alex, "Laura, you're there. Park in the lot to your right. And good luck. We'll be here with you every step of the way."

*

Miguel peeked out of the window. Paul was looking at him intensely. He sensed a change in Miguel's internal dialogue, so he probed a bit more. He knew Laura would show up at any minute, so he had to try to figure something out. He thought some distraction might work, and maybe there was a chance he could make everything okay.

"Miguel, when did you first know you had this gift?"

Miguel turned, looked at Paul, and despite the wry smile demonstrating he knew what Paul was trying to accomplish, he answered. "Huh. No one's ever asked me that."

Paul remained hopeful.

"I had a shitty childhood. I had shitty parents. I had shitty friends. Basically, I lived in constant shit."

"How so, Miguel?"

"My parents were never home. Then were second generation from Brazil and did quite well for themselves. We had a lot of money and a big house. I was an only kid. Frankly they gave me everything."

"So, what was the problem?"

"When I was ten, my uncle used to babysit me. Like, all the time. This one night, that son of a bitch got drunk. He, well, you know ... did ... bad stuff." Miguel swallowed hard.

Paul sensed where the anger came from.

"He. Well, he, touched me. He made me do things to him that no one deserves to be made to do ... why the hell am I telling you this?"

Paul knew he had to be careful here. "Man, I'm sorry. People suck. People are assholes and can be horrific."

Miguel turned away and started to laugh. "I'm glad it happened. Otherwise, I would have probably never found out this gift I have. Let me tell you what I did to that bastard!"

Paul's heart sank, but at least he felt he was preoccupying him, though he feared that he may have been revving Miguel to another level.

"When my parents came home that same night, and my uncle left, I was in the room, sore, mentally and physically. I wanted to kill everyone. I wanted to end my life. And of course, I wanted to kill my uncle. But also, my asshole parents put me in this situation. They left me fending for myself, and I know they wouldn't have believed me. I remember it like it was yesterday. I was lying in bed, fuming. That's when I screamed out the words ... I screamed so loudly; I still remember them vividly."

Paul swallowed hard. He had a feeling what was coming next.

"I said, I hope my goddamn uncle breaks his neck."

Miguel was smiling, and Paul was horrified.

"And that's all I said. It felt cathartic. I felt better, and I went to sleep right away. It was strange. But I felt better."

Paul's experience with glowers was that when they hexed someone, it could be days or even weeks before something happened. But he had a feeling that Miguel might be the exception.

"The next morning, I woke up hearing my mom crying. She's sobbing uncontrollably. I walked out of the room and asked Dad what's going on."

Miguel was almost bouncing around the room, though Paul noted that he was still mostly avoiding the window. He was smiling and recollecting what seemed like a sweet and lovely memory that he would never forget; Paul was mortified.

"And Dad says, 'Son, I'm sorry but your uncle was in an accident on his way home from babysitting you last night.' So, I ask my dad, what happened? I just had to contain my excitement. My dad said with a heavy heart, 'He is alive, but he can't and won't be able to move any part of his body. He hurt his spine badly."

Miguel looked like he was floating on a cloud. He was smiling recalling his great accomplishment. A lifelong path of destruction was sown from that fateful day. Paul had wished that Miguel's uncle was a paraplegic before he decided to molest Miguel. Then maybe this day would be different.

"I hung my head. I hugged my dad. I hugged my mom. And I think I deserved an Oscar for that. I ran into my room and knew; I just knew I had the ability to fuck people up. I was so happy. My uncle was a bastard, and he deserved it. Even then, the morning after he touched me, I wanted to call him up and thank him for doing it. And I did, many times! Every single time I saw that asshole, right before he died a few years ago, I whispered in his ear, 'Thank you for hurting me, man, otherwise you would never be in this chair.'" Paul hated his uncle for what he did; for the monster he created.

CHAPTER 26

Laura parked her car. Earlier she had rolled her window down to get much-needed air; the gentle warm breeze stroked her face and calmed her. The calm before the storm, she thought. Much like the overcast sky, she was not sure what the next few minutes had in store for her. LJ was talking in her ear, but she could not really focus on the conversation. She sensed the tingling in her feet and slightly itching scalp. She realized she had not showered in quite some time. She let out a little chuckle that did not feel funny.

"Are you okay?" Alex asked Laura. She knew what he really wanted, for her to come back and not go through with this godforsaken plan.

Laura shook her head and lied to Alex. "Everything's going to be okay. I've got this."

Her attempt did not make her feel any more secure, and she assumed Alex felt similarly.

"Remember, we're right here with you."

*

Alex was not calm anymore, at least not internally. His head spun and his feet restless. The world seemed totally messed up, and he felt this was the start of a total change to his life going forward. He dreaded what that meant to him. He also felt like he was boiling up. He turned up the air conditioning to find some relief. He hoped that he would not glow, but at this point in time, he did not care if LJ found out he was a glower; this was about Laura, and that was all Alex could really focus on.

LJ spoke once again. She was repeating herself, and Alex and Laura were both thankful. They were deep inside their own thoughts.

"Laura, to recap, get him near that window. Do not make him mad. Listen to him, and try to be empathetic. Don't engage with Paul. Listen to Miguel. Hear him. Get him to trust you. And get him to that window. We'll do the rest."

"Okay."

Laura got out of the car.

*

Miguel's phone buzzed. He hastily had set up several mini-video devices to warn him of incoming visitors, including one by the stairs on this floor, and the other by the front door. He was rather amused at his good fortune. He had been monitoring Paul for a few weeks, but after he went missing, he was about to give up. It felt like a wasted trip, but when he was at the airport, he not only saw Laura and Paul, but he saw LJ and her men. It was an opportunity to have some fun and get back at LJ the best way he could think of. He was grateful for the opportunity after so many years of trying. He was not sure what would ultimately happen by the end of the day, but he was internally buoyed by the chance to unleash hell on LJ—in some fashion, at least.

He was also careful not to let Paul see that he knew they were coming; Paul could easily end this fun by yelling and warning Laura it was a trap. But of course, Miguel knew that Laura was aware that indeed, it was a trap. And he knew that she and her friend Alex and LJ would also have a plan. He was very curious about Alex. He did not seem to have any relationship with Laura besides friendship, nor any gifts. Nevertheless, he was not the threat; that was LJ's modus operandi. And he was ready for it all. In fact, he was ready to make them all pay if that's what it came down to. That's what it was going to come down to if all the pieces fell into place. Miguel's excitement rose with every passing minute.

Miguel saw three cars in the past ten minutes near his building. Two were parked at the adjacent building's parking lot. Fortunately, there was only one way into that building's parking lot, and his cameras could pick them up. One of LJ's men went into that adjacent building. *Probably a sniper*, Miguel thought. LJ was obviously here with her assholes, as he suspected. This made Miguel quite content; he wanted revenge today.

He considered closing the shades to the only window in the small office, but what was the fun in that? Plus, he considered that would completely trigger them to try and storm the office. He knew Laura would try and lure him toward the window. The excitement was nearly unbearable for Miguel. He just wanted it to start already!

The second car sat in the adjacent parking lot, and though the picture was blurry, he could see two people who stayed sat in the car. He assumed LJ and Alex. He was not sure how LJ might have gotten here with Laura and Alex, especially after what they did to Paul, but he knew that LJ was a mastermind and a manipulator. And that was all the better. Have them working together and deal with them all here at this point was more than he could wish for.

He observed one man dressed in black hide behind his building. That was the one he really had to worry about. But he had Paul and soon enough Laura, and that was enough leverage to get out of this unscathed. If not, all hell would break loose. Of course, LJ was the real prize; he needed to get her above all else. The door to the office was heavy enough to withstand a few kicks, so he would have time to react. *All is right with the world*, he thought. *This is going to be fun.*

*

Laura walked to the door of the office building. Her feet hurt, and her hands felt thick. Her breathing was rapid, and her head and brain were heavy. She assumed that adrenaline would be pumping through her body, but the fatigue she felt at that moment said otherwise; she had been on maximum stress for hours now. She thought to herself that how she felt might be something that heart attack or stroke victims experience. It would be terrifying if not for the unfathomable situation she was already walking into.

She also thought it would be slightly ironic to drop dead right then and there before she even got into the goddamn building.

For better or worse, she entered. She knew Miguel and Paul were on the third floor, but she was told by LJ to call Miguel once she entered. He had to at least have some doubt about whether she came alone. She took out her phone, dialed the preprogrammed number, and took a deep breath.

"Is this my new favorite friend?"

Miguel's voice was startling. In another world, this would be the way a best friend would pick up the phone before a night on the town. But this was no night on the town. Laura froze for a second.

"You're okay, Laura," LJ said in her ear.

Laura thought that she could never be comforted by LJ, but she was wrong. Her body immediately let out a sigh. Laura realized LJ was an enigma. She was probably a sociopath with a hero syndrome but most definitely a madwoman doing batshit crazy things on people. But right now, it was comforting.

"Hello, Laura. You don't want to say hi?" Miguel sounded impatient.

"I'm here, Miguel. I'm here."

*

Alex was breathing heavily. His legs were fidgeting, but he stayed quiet so he would not bother Laura's likely fragile state. He felt useless. He was looking at the camera, half wondering why the picture on LJ's tablet was so steady. Laura was walking slowly, giving a great view of the office building foyer. Alex was starting to feel very warm inside. Not the good warm feeling when Laura had touched his hand just little while ago. Not the type of feeling you get when things are going well and you're in a state of flow. No, it was a burning sensation. His skin was itching and burning at the same time.

He recalled feeling like this when he was in Boston for school. He and Laura finished class on a Friday evening in early February. It was absolutely the coldest day he had felt in a long time, and they wanted to hit a local pub a few blocks from class. Their walk was horrendously freezing, and when they entered the pub, they hit a wall of heat radiating from the massive fireplace. Within seconds, Alex was ripping his gloves, hat, coat, and sweater off. Laura was laughing at him. It was no doubt a funny scene, but Alex was burning up inside. The sudden wave of heat from that fireplace made it almost unbearable to breathe.

This is how he felt at this moment. LJ touched his shoulder. "Are you okay, Alex." She had pressed the mute button. Alex saw that Laura had stopped mid-foyer and picked up her cell phone.

"I'm okay, I'm just feeling a bit ... warm."

"Don't worry. It's going to be okay. Laura's one in a million. She'll play this out fine, and in no time, she'll be back here with us."

Alex briefly considered that LJ had been replaced with another person. In the past couple of hours, she had acted like a caring, empathetic person. Not a controlling, unsympathetic psychopath. He liked this person much better, despite his many reservations about her character.

"You're okay, Laura." Alex looked at LJ, looked at the screen, took a deep breath, and wanted to rip his sweat covered shirt off. Instead, he turned the air conditioner to the lowest degree setting and the speed up several notches.

*

Paul was uncomfortable. Pain pulsed on his forehead where Miguel had hit him earlier, but the internal anguish he felt was overriding almost all of his senses. Paul wondered what the plan was. The window was an option and he had hoped a very limited one given his head and torso covered nearly all of it. He assumed Laura had a weapon to try to stop Miguel, though she was not trained and generally never approved of them. She has always avoided any marksmanship lessons or self-defense classes. He cursed himself for not pushing her more to do that in the past.

Paul started to think back to the years he spent with Laura. She was so beautiful and smart and interesting. She was quiet but not shy. She held a confidence about her that made people want to be around her and yet she rarely had friends. She did not need a lot of attention, and that made her even more appealing to him. He yearned for those moments and wished he could be back in them. He knew, though, even on the remote chance they both could get out of this alive, she would never go back to him. In her eyes, no doubt, he ruined everything by excluding her and effectively going behind her back. Paul felt more heartbreak about losing her than about his likely death. He just wished she had never come for him.

Miguel's phone rang, and Paul's personal self-pity party temporarily ceased, though the growing knot in his stomach did not. It was Laura, and Miguel was beaming. Paul felt defeated, but a glimmer of hope entered his mind. Maybe Laura would be his savior. And maybe there was a chance for him and Laura to get out of this alive.

*

Laura did not take the elevator. It was only two floors, and while she had plenty of time to think, she wanted more. She was walking into a pit of fire. She could feel it. Her thoughts were all over the place, but the window would be her salvation, she hoped.

When she got to the third floor, she stopped before she opened the door to the hallway.

"Alex?" she asked quietly. Alex was standing by and immediately responded, "Yes, Laura?"

"I'm scared. I have to do this, but I'm really scared. I have you in my life again. My parents and I are back together. There are no real secrets in my life anymore, and I feel for the first time almost whole." Laura's voice was trembling again. Alex never heard anything like that mutual hope and resignation from Laura before. It scared him, and it made him furious. *That fucking Miguel*, he thought. Alex had his own fear coursing throughout his body, but it was slowly building into a wave of anger.

"Hey, everything's going to be fine. We're here. Remember, the window. If he doesn't go there, LJ's man will be right outside the door."

As he spoke, he realized that this plan was hardly satisfactory. Laura should not be there. He knew that this was likely going to be a disaster. He wondered quietly why they did not call the police but knew that Miguel's words alone could cause a massacre. Alex was burning up inside.

"Okay, Alex. I'm going in. And ..."

"Yeah?"

"And ... I ..." Alex could hear Laura's voice crack. He did not want her to lose it.

"Don't worry, Laura, everything is going to be all right."

"Alex, I ... I ... I love you."

A wave of emotions poured through Alex, bringing him on the verge of losing control.

"I always have. I just needed you to know that. Just in case. And I'm sorry I ran away from you. You were always the one, but I was afraid. I'm so sorry."

Alex brushed away the tears dripping down his cheeks. His heart swelled while his anger tremored throughout his pores.

"Laura, thank you. And I ..."

Before Alex could say it back, Laura said, "Okay, I'm going in. Talk soon."

*

LJ looked at Alex. She was smiling slightly in the way a mother smiles proudly at her child. Alex still did not fully trust LJ but felt something was different with her on this trip in hell. But he couldn't focus on that now. He mouthed her to press mute. She did.

"The sniper guy is in place, right?"

She nodded.

"And the other guy is going into the building, right?"

She pointed to the table, swiped a screen, and another video popped up. The "goon," as he and Laura used to call them, was entering the building slowly. Alex nodded and took a large gulp of air.

"Okay, good. LJ, please let them know that they can't fuck this up."

*

Miguel's tablet buzzed again. Laura was waiting by the stairwell door. Miguel always thought that Laura was gorgeous, even that fateful day at the football game years ago. He understood why Paul was with her; he longed for her many times throughout the years.

A second buzz. One of LJ's henchmen just entered the building. Miguel's excitement was growing by the second; he thought of how he smashed one of LJ's men head back when he was her captive; he wanted to do it again.

Another buzz and a quick swipe of the tablet screen saw Laura enter the third floor. She walked slowly straight ahead. Miguel had taped an arrow on a wall to indicate where to go; he did not have time to be sophisticated, and while he was slightly amused at this oversimplification, he thought it would avoid wasting time for Laura knocking other office doors. Laura was now at the door; Miguel's heart was racing with anticipation.

*

Laura opened the stairwell door and noticed there were three directions; left, straight, and right. LJ had already told her it was straight, but that was apparently unnecessary after she looked at the taped wall.

"You see this, guys?"

Alex and LJ responded together, "We do."

Laura kept moving forward. Her hands felt tingly and tight, and she really had to pee. Her natural instincts told her to turn around, go down the stairs, and run. Run. *Run.*

Then she heard a click. She turned around quickly and figured it was likely the stairwell door. Before she could say anything, LJ spoke.

"Laura, don't say anything. Miguel is watching you. We don't want him knowing you can hear us and we can see him. Just slowly turn around and keep walking toward the office. It's our guy behind you."

Laura did as LJ asked. She thought back to the fateful night in Hoover, Alabama. A young girl looking to figure shit out running on a football field to try and save someone's life that she knew nothing about. The internal struggle to help someone who was not her father, who she ultimately could not help. She wished she never ran onto that field; heck, she wished she never got on the plane to Alabama. She realized she should have just talked more with her dad back then; she wished she had the wisdom and the nerve. She was filled with fear and regret.

She placed her hand on the doorknob. It was trembling while her mind was spinning.

*

LJ pointed to her tablet and spoke to one of her guys. "Mark, Laura is at the door. I think he has small cameras located throughout."

"Yes, I saw them."

"Be careful."

"What is going on?" Alex asked.

"It looks like Miguel can see our guy coming in. We might have to rely on the window."

Alex first nodded in agreement and then defensively, with fear in his heart, shook his head.

"We're going to be fine, Alex. I believe in Laura."

Alex believed in Laura too. But expecting Laura to handle this situation was foolhardy. Alex swallowed hard and tried to breathe deeply. His heart was pounding out of his chest.

CHAPTER 27

The time was here. There was no turning back now. Laura laid her hand on the cold doorknob and turned. Before she could barely turn her wrist, the door swung open. Straight ahead was Paul, looking at her with fear and shame. Tied to a chair, he looked like death warmed over. Her heart broke for him.

"Get in now, Laura!" Miguel shouted from behind the door. He had his gun fixed on Laura's head. Laura walked reluctantly through the door. Miguel kicked the door, and it slammed behind her, and then he pointed to Paul and said, "Get over there with Paul." Laura again obeyed him. Miguel quickly locked the door. Laura was next to Paul but kept her gaze on Miguel. There was a foul odor in the room; she could not put words to it except that it smelled and felt like death. A shiver crept from her lower back to the top of her head.

Now that they were barricaded in the small office, Laura noticed that Miguel had relaxed. He was almost ruefully smiling at Laura, but she knew there was likely no regret in anything related to Miguel. Laura still had not looked at Paul and had remained quiet. Only Miguel seemed to be enjoying the moment. Finally, Laura gathered up the courage and spoke. "Miguel, what is going on?"

Miguel observed her not in the way one looks at an enemy but one of admiration for a fellow patriot. Of respect. Of longing. Laura did not like it. Miguel than began to scan her uncomfortably. Paul interjected, "Miguel, can you just answer her question?" Paul's voice was fragile. Laura finally looked at Paul and nearly lost her balance. She saw a ghost of a man who she had been with for nearly ten years. A driven person who desperately wanted to be a hero. She had left him not long ago for that very reason, but right now, right here, she loved him for it.

Miguel's face sank a little. His eyes narrowed, and his lips pursed up against his teeth.

"I'm not your son, Paul." He looked amused but impatient.

Paul persisted. "Please, she came and she's alone, can you..."

"Shut your goddamn mouth, little man. Let the grownups talk." Miguel's amused look went straight to rage.

Paul swallowed hard. Laura swallowed harder. Miguel let out an almost hysterical laugh.

*

LJ and Alex were watching and listening. When Laura turned to Paul after he spoke, they both recoiled slightly. Paul looked beaten physically, spiritually, and emotionally. Alex wanted to tear into LJ for her part in this. Had she not done this to Paul herself, they all might be in a different, and most likely a much safer predicament. But he had to concern himself with the here and now.

"Jesus Christ, LJ. This is not good."

LJ nodded. She checked in with both of her guys. The sniper kept saying the same thing, negative on the target, and the one in the office was still trying to figure out how to get the door open without scaring Miguel into doing something stupid.

"Laura's just going to need to get him to the window. Or keep him sane until we can get Mark in there ..."

Alex became less assured of the plan with each passing moment. Horrible scenarios rang through his mind. Miguel could easily kill them both and escape before anyone could even get on the second floor. He was getting angry again at the helplessness he felt. He wished he were there with Laura, though he did not think he could really help.

LJ laid a hand once again on Alex. "You have to relax. Remember, you losing control won't help here. Breathe, and try to keep cool; we'll get through this."

Alex thought about that first time he glowed in front of Laura. Despite the fact she looked terrified, he still saw kindness in her face. It was a curse to her. And right now, it was a curse to him that he could not use it. He wished he could, and he could not care less if LJ found him out. But, even if he could, it would not help - Miguel was impervious to his glow. Though he eventually accepted the potential devastation of his ability to others, he was nonetheless, now, in the biggest moment of his life, powerless to protect the one person he cared for the most.

*

"So, how are you? It's been so long. Like what, ten years?"

Laura nodded. *How in the world could he be so nonchalant?*

"So?" he pushed.

LJ whispered in Laura's ear. "Talk to him, Laura. Keep him talking."

"Miguel, it was such a long time ago."

He smiled. "Yes, indeed. I can recall you running that field like it was on fire. You kind of ruined a moment for me, though." He chuckled a little too loudly and not so pleasantly. "But that's all right. I still got that asshole referee afterwards," Miguel said proudly. Both Paul and Laura felt nauseated.

"But you know what is the worst part, Laura? It's that you and your boyfriend here spied on me for years. What the fuck? And I could do nothing to you or him. I tried to screw you both up, but nothing would happen, no matter how hard I tried. It was first time I realized that I couldn't touch you damn sensers. That was too bad. But I guess it all worked out in the end."

Laura was taken aback at Miguel's hatred. She thought it best to defuse with some hard reality. "I know we interfered with you. But we didn't actually do anything. We scoped you out for a few years, always keeping our distance. We never talked to you, and only spied on you in public. And we gave up years ago because we didn't see you do anything. To us, you were basically a reformed glower. So, we left you alone. That was years ago!"

Miguel was stoic. He seemed to be hearing Laura, or so she hoped.

"Yeah, you're right. You did. But you know what? Guess who didn't stop? LJ!"

Laura breathed deeply. He was right and she knew that. She pleaded with Miguel. "But I didn't even know her till recently, Miguel. What does she have to do with Paul and I?"

"Funny you ask that. See, when LJ was testing me, much like she was testing Paul, I got out. Like Paul did. Except, I decided that I was going to give her something to remember me by. I went searching for her and her thugs. I got into a surveillance room." He grinned, eyes maliciously alight, "You're right; I had no real reason to involve you or Paul. But that was before I saw the pictures on the wall in that surveillance room."

Laura was uncertain where Miguel was going with this, but she felt it was not a place she wanted to be. He was connecting dots she did not know were connected.

"They had you and Paul's mugs on the wall. Underneath that they had a description called *Their Surveillance*. And the first picture on that wall was me. *Me!*"

He was getting more agitated, and Laura felt things spiraling fast.

"But, we didn't do anything. We didn't tell LJ anything. We didn't give her information, and ..."

"You fucking didn't have to!" Miguel shouted.

"Once she caught wind of you two, she did her own surveillance. Basically, everything you know, she knows. So, if you had stopped following me after that football game, who knows. I might have reformed. I might have changed. And I would not have been almost killed by that bitch. So, it's your fault! She knew about me because of you two assholes."

Laura was about to continue to plead her case when Paul interrupted.

"Laura is innocent in this. She never wanted any of this. She didn't want anyone to get hurt. She wanted to *help* you. She wanted to talk to *you*. Then she wanted us to leave you alone. It's not her fault."

Laura looked at Paul and mouthed "shush." Paul did not stop.

"So, please, let her go. Your beef is with me. Well really, it's with LJ, but have it with me. Not Laura."

Miguel was amused. "Laura, push Paul over here so I can talk to him better."

The window. *The goddamn window.* Laura totally forgot about trying to get Miguel over to it.

"No, you come over here and talk to me," Paul said. Miguel was visibly getting pissed. Paul and Laura could see a low light emanating from Miguel's body. While they understood he could not hurt them via his curse, it sent a fear slithering through them both. Laura realized that Paul had a suspicion of the window, and apparently Miguel was already in the know.

"Bring him over to me now!" Miguel shouted, glowing ever more slightly.

*

LJ and Alex's eyes transfixed on the screen, feeling less useful with each passing moment. Alex was fearful like he had never been. That fear was eclipsing his anger. For now.

"Miguel knows we're trying to lure him to the window."

"Yes." LJ reached out to Frank, the sniper. No clear shot; he could only see Laura and Paul. Mark was still alert though had not entered the third-floor hallway. LJ told him to be ready to run to the office fast when he was needed.

"Laura, just keep him talking," LJ said calmly, but it was the first time that Alex sensed fear in her voice. He was burning up inside. Though the air-conditioned car showed sixty degrees, sweat bubbled on his forehead, and he could feel his shirt caked to the sweat on his back. He started to feel anger coming from his feet; he glanced at LJ and tried to keep calm, but he knew deep down inside, he would soon be found out. It didn't matter. It was nothing compared to what Laura and Paul were going through.

*

Laura did not react to Miguel's command. She felt if she did, she would lose Paul and probably herself to his madness. Instead, she tried to lower Miguel's anger; though she knew the words she would speak were utter nonsense.

"Talk to me. What do you want? Do you really want to do this? You have done nothing wrong. No one is waiting by the door to bring you into the cops. You could literally walk out of here and just leave. We could all leave and be done with this forever."

Miguel was glowing brightly. He brought the pistol up to chest height, pointed at Laura. Laura closed her eyes and reflexively turned her body. And then a blast. Her ears burned. She froze in place, waiting for the pain to kick in. Instead, Paul let out a horrifying shriek. She opened her eyes and saw a hole that spurted blood from Paul's left leg. She turned to Miguel, who had finally stopped glowing.

"Bring him over now, or I'll shoot him in the head. Do it *now!*"

Laura grabbed the bottom of the chair and, surprising herself, nearly lifted Paul off the floor and dragged him to Miguel.

"Now, that wasn't that hard, was it, Laura?"

Paul was whimpering, and Laura was distraught. She wondered where LJ's men were, and yet she also feared that if they barged into the room she would be shot before they could help. She wanted Miguel dead; he was no longer fit for this world.

As the machinations of the moment were churning in Laura's head, Miguel walked slowly behind Paul. With a gun in his left hand now, he raised his right hand to Paul's throat. Laura blinked hard and could not grasp what was happening. She knew it was a small knife, but she couldn't move or say anything. She was frozen with fear. Before she could scream "Stop," Paul's throat was open. Blood gushed out like she had never seen before. Paul's eyes were wide open in terror and staring directly at Laura. With tears rolling down his face, he tried to reach out to her. He moved to the side as much as possible and pushed his bound hands ever so slightly toward her. She reached and held his shoulder and started to cry. She saw Paul's hopeless expression and she was horrified. She saw his life lowly fade until his body lurched forward, gasping for air. But no air was found, and Paul's head fell forward.

CHAPTER 28

Alex had watched what unfolded while in major dysphoria. It was all happening way too fast. He could hear LJ frantically yelling at her two cohorts. It was like an out-of-body experience for Alex, though not an angelic one.

He had not known Paul that well, but he had just witnessed his life tragically and too quickly diminish into nothingness. Alex could not feel for Paul this moment; there would be time for that. Laura was his greatest concern. He was feeling nauseated, and his skin was on fire, scared he would soon lose his mind.

"LJ," Alex pleaded, "what are we going to do?"

LJ took a deep breath and kept talking to her guys. She sounded frantic and looked worse. It did not ease Alex's already fragile state.

Back at the tablet screen, he heard Miguel demand, "Get on your knees, Laura."

Alex's stomach, head, and body convulsed. He was staring at a certain trainwreck, and he felt his life would never, ever be the same.

*

"Get on your knees, Laura."

Laura looked away from Paul toward Miguel in a state of shock. She did not really hear what Miguel had said.

"Why ... why ... why did you do that? What ... what kind of monster are you?" Miguel looked at Laura with a madman's smile, one that knew he was in control and

loving every minute of his debauchery. Laura was appalled and felt terror in every part of her being. She knew she would be dead soon.

"Get on your knees Laura. Now!"

Laura had come to grips that she would die. Right now. Right here. She had made many mistakes in her life, and coming here was the worst one. Maybe if she had stayed away, Paul would be alive. Before she walked to Miguel, she realized she had the knife. Her brain was not functioning normally, but she knew this was the last chance.

"Okay, I'm coming over"

Laura slowly walked toward Miguel with her head down. She slid her hand behind her back and up her shirt; LJ had put attached the knife to her belt. She grabbed the end and held it tight. Within two feet of Miguel, Laura lifted her head up at the psychopathic, murdering devil in front of her. Miguel was smiling but with eyes narrowed; this was her chance.

She swung her arm around and thrusted the knife toward Miguel's throat. Miguel stepped back and easily dodged Laura. He then immediately swung his gun and hit Laura in the head. Her knife flew across the room and she dropped to her knees.

"Laura. Laura. Now, why did you have to go and do that? You're not as nice as people think you are, huh? Now you've made me even more pissed off!" Miguel spoke as if he were a teacher or parent, tasking the child to do better. He was glowing brighter than she'd ever seen.

Laura resigned herself, knowing the end was near. She waited for the sound of a trigger, and then she expected a shot of pain. Then nothing. She took one final breath, clenched, and waited.

Then she heard a quiet growling sound. She recognized that sound but just couldn't put a name to it. Then she realized what it was. A zipper. She heard the words, "You know what you have to do, Laura. And be careful down there. You don't want to a fucking bullet in your brain, do you?"

*

"Get on your knees, Laura."

Alex looked in horror. Everything around Alex felt quiet. He was sure it was shock. It was almost as if he were suspended from his surroundings. He was not quite sure what was happening to his mental state, but despite the quietness, he was frozen with fear.

Then Miguel hit Laura. Alex felt an immediate rush sweep over, back and through him. He thought at this moment in time he would explode and at best go bat shit crazy. He looked at the screen and listened, and while the car was silent, it felt like a barrage of explosions was happening all around him.

Laura's failed attempt to stab the son of a bitch was not unexpected. Alex knew it would likely not work. After Miguel hit Laura, Alex convulsed again; he knew he was about to pass out, and he silently cursed himself, knowing he was not there for Laura when she needed him the most.

Then he heard what sounded like a zipper and saw Miguel lower his jeans. Alex immediately lost consciousness.

*

LJ was frantically trying to get updates from Mark and Frank. With them both at the door in the stairwell, they finally rushed to the office door. LJ told them to stand down by the door and await further instructions. She waited until there was a chance Miguel would be distracted enough for them to shoot their way in. She just had to make sure she and they would not get Laura killed. And then she saw Miguel drop his jeans.

Before she could fully turn and look at Alex, she was blinded by a sudden explosion of light. She was not shocked that Alex was a glower; she had come to assume he might be, since Laura had a deep connection with him. But this was a different type of light; she had seen a lot of glowers "light up" in her time, but this was very dissimilar. This illumination had a red tinge, like that of a burning sun. It burned and radiated so brightly, LJ could not see or speak or think of the impending doom facing Laura.

*

Laura heard Miguel shout, "Get moving, you whore!" She knew she was in shock. She thought of

Paul, next to her, tied to a chair behind her - dead. She visualized Alex sitting in the car probably losing his mind and wondered if he would ever be the same once she died. Her parents would struggle to move on and mourn the potential of what could have been with the new family knowledge of the past few days. Yes, she knew she was in shock, but her mind's eye was able to process the what-ifs and what would never be. She leveled her breathing and took a deep breath. Her sobbing, which she only now realized, had stopped. She steeled herself and knew that she had to do what she had to do, though it likely didn't matter.

And then she felt something drip on her head.

Laura was disgusted beyond anything she ever knew she could feel. While she thanked the Lord that she didn't have to touch that devil, she felt nauseous from what had dripped off his horrifying body. The son of bitch could not even wait. She thought of Alex again and became sad for him that he had to witness Miguel releasing upon her.

More of the same dripped on her scalp, and it started to feel heavy. Laura's stomach turned furiously, and she thought she might puke, though she resisted. More drops hit her head, but this time it felt more like a flow. Her eyes were still closed and did not move. She felt forever traumatized, but a move might be enough to end her life.

She did think it odd that she heard nothing from Miguel. Maybe he was laughing silently, finishing off strong and then finishing off Laura as the final exclamation point. She finally could not stand it anymore and almost involuntarily moved to her left. She reluctantly opened up her eyes slightly and squinted at Miguel, fully expecting to see his horrifying smile with his grotesque dick in his hand and proud of dismantling any shred of dignity in Laura.

But what she saw was more horrifying.

*

Alex's internal blindness subsided quickly. He felt disoriented, and his head was pounding. It was the worst migraine he had ever felt; he was barely able to think, and the pain was nearly unbearable. He knew he was out only for a few seconds, but for a moment, he was unsure of where he was. As he glanced at LJ, who was strangely holding both of her hands against her eyes, the circumstances of the day rushed like a freight train through his brain. He immediately looked back at the tablet with a sense of dread, but what he saw confused him. Laura was still on her knees, while Miguel, still standing though wide-eyed fear emanated from him, with a fountain of blood gushing from his nose, eyes, and ears.

*

Laura saw blood run cleanly from Miguel's head, dripping fast down on his shoulders. And his wide eyes, terrified beyond comprehension, were full of hemoglobin tears. Laura bolted away from Miguel but remained fixated on his eyes. She was dumbfounded, mystified, still scared shitless, but finally a sense of hope filled her body.

Miguel clasped his throat. He could not breathe. He dropped to his bare knees and tried to scream. He reached out for Laura. Laura could tell it was a reach for help, but she instinctively moved backward, further away from him. She noticed that the gun was still in his hand. Miguel noticed her glance and realizing the same thing, pointing the gun at her head.

Laura closed her eyes, steadied herself for imminent death. She again thought about her mom, the lovely and caring mother who was wonderful. Her dad, and all that he went through. Her best friend in the world and would-be lover for life, Alex. She breathed one final time with absolute knowledge that it was over. Though, instead of a gunshot, she heard a loud thump. She opened her eyes and saw Miguel on the ground, wide eyed and dead.

CHAPTER 29

Fred and Mary were unusually doting. Laura was sitting at the table with Alex to her left. She was smiling, reveling in the attention that her parents were giving them both. It was unusual, especially from her father.

"Dad, we're fine. Come sit with us and relax."

Fred came to Laura and softly kissed her forehead.

"We'll be back soon. We have to go grab a couple of things at the store that we forgot. And get more wine. We all deserve more wine."

"Thanks, Dad." Fred had insisted that Alex call him Dad. It was still strange coming from his tongue, but he was getting used to it. Fred had also kissed Alex on the top of his head. Alex blushed. Laura chuckled.

"Stop laughing at your dad; he wasn't always this cool and stoic." Mary's comment made them all laugh, and Alex snorted some of his beer. Fred shook his head, grabbed Mary's hand, and led them out of the house.

Laura collected herself while Alex wiped away the beer running from his nose.

"This is so not what I thought your parents would be like."

Laura nodded in agreement. "Well, the past two months have been a blessing. They are just so ..." Laura stopped. Alex could see she was getting flustered. The past few weeks were not easy for any of them. But Laura was the most affected. Alex had been by her side almost the entirety of it; he could not help himself and was nearly afraid to leave her, and Laura did not seem to mind.

"I'm so sorry all of this happened, Laura. I'm just so sorry."

Laura held Alex's hand, leaned into him, and kissed him softly. "No, Alex, you saved my life. You saved me from that bastard."

Alex was not sure what really happened. They had talked about it a few times, but normally, Laura avoided it. Today was different.

"Can you remember what happened, honey?"

Alex thought a moment before replying to Laura. "You know, it was all a big blur. But I remember rage. And burning. But mostly rage. Rage that I hadn't ever thought was possible. I remember seeing ..." Alex swallowed hard, looking for confirmation from Laura that he could and should go on. She nodded and held his hand.

"I remember almost losing my mind when I saw him kill Paul. But when he pointed the gun at you and then dropped his ... well, his pants, I lost consciousness."

Laura nodded. She understood how traumatic it was. She was there, and she could barely recall the details.

"They said it was a massively ruptured aneurysm. They never saw anything like it at the morgue. They also said it was the luckiest coincidence."

Alex nodded in agreement. He felt, or rather knew he was responsible for Miguel's death.

"But how in the world could that have happened? I mean, LJ has stated that in the decades she's been studying this, it has never happened."

Alex now shook his head. He did not understand how he was able to do it.

"Or maybe it was one giant coincidence?"

Alex then nodded but answered, "I wish I could believe that, but I don't think that is the case."

"In any event, Alex, you saved my life. Thank you for that."

Alex grabbed the back of her neck, brought her closer, and kissed her passionately. When they stopped, Alex asked Laura, "Have you heard from LJ?"

Laura shook her head.

"Not since that day" Laura answered and then asked, "You?"

Alex nodded in affirmation. It surprised Laura.

"Yeah, she sent me an email a couple weeks ago. I have not yet responded to her. I did not want to stress you out, or me for that matter. Want me to read it to you now?" Laura nodded again. Alex grabbed his phone, opened his email app, and began.

"Hi, Alex. I hope you and Laura are doing well and recovering as best you can. I am sorry we couldn't help Paul and also for not being much support to you and Laura. I wish I could have done more. Thank you for doing what you did; twenty plus years dealing with this stuff, and I never thought it was possible. Take care of yourselves and your family. LJ."

Laura listened and kept silent. She still was not sure about LJ. She wanted to believe in LJ, but there was a large nagging voice in the back of her brain that said "move on." Alex felt the same. After a few moments, Laura spoke. "Well, that is that. I'm happy to have you in my life finally, and my parents are healthy and safe. Let's be thankful for that and live a normal life. Let's try and get back all those lost years together. Let's get over what happened and just ... move on."

Alex smiled softly and kissed her lips.

Their phones buzzed simultaneously. They picked them up and read the same message from LJ.

"Guys, I have found another Miguel. I need your help."

THE END